The Other Madden

There is oil on Madden land and Bren Deavers means to have it. But when Joe Madden is killed and sent home wrapped in barbed wire, things heat up. For the Maddens are fighters and Elmira and Emily are going to do just that.

But Joe also had a brother. One nobody talked about. The dangerous one.

They just referred to him as – the other Madden!

By the same author
Lightning Strike!

Writing as B.S. Dunn
Fury at Bent Fork
Brolin
Brothers of the Gun

Writing as Sam Clancy
Valley of Thunder
Even Marshals Hang!
The Man Who Burned Hell!
Hellraiser!

The Other Madden

Brent Towns

A Black Horse Western

ROBERT HALE

© Brent Towns 2019
First published in Great Britain 2019

ISBN 978-0-7198-2918-5

The Crowood Press
The Stable Block
Crowood Lane
Ramsbury
Marlborough
Wiltshire SN8 2HR

www.bhwesterns.com

Robert Hale is an imprint
of The Crowood Press

The right of Brent Towns to be identified as
author of this work has been asserted by him
in accordance with the Copyright, Designs and
Patents Act 1988
Typeset by
Derek Doyle & Associates, Shaw Heath
Printed and bound in Great Britain by
4Bind Ltd, Stevenage, SG1 2XT

This one is for Sam and Jacob.
And for all the cowboys we've lost in the past couple of years.
The genre won't be the same without y'all.

CHAPTER 1

I didn't want to shoot the guard – tried hard to avoid it, in fact – but he left twenty-eight-year-old Trace Madden, me, no choice, and the Colt .45 in my fist roared an instant before the sawn-off shotgun could come level and blow my guts out all over the dusty stage road.

The slug smashed into the guard's right shoulder and spun him around, the shotgun in his hands discharging harmlessly into the brush at the side of the road.

The sudden explosion startled some crows from a nearby cottonwood, and with a raucous protest they flew into the clear afternoon sky.

'What the hell?' one of the three outlaws with me blurted out. 'Of all the stupid, idiotic things to do . . . I oughta just finish him off right now, boss, and be done with him.'

The speaker behind the pulled-up kerchief was named Frenchy, a short, wiry man who came from Kansas. The other two outlaws who currently held the driver and passengers under their cocked guns were named Blaze and Miller.

Blaze was a tall, solidly built man like I was. But unlike my dark hair, Blaze's was blond. Both of us, however, were fast with a six-gun. Blindingly so.

Nobody had ever asked Blaze where he came from. All we knew was that it wasn't New Mexico, our current location.

The third man, Miller, came from Texas. He was a tall, lanky drifter who'd been down on his luck when I'd found him in a saloon in Socorro.

Myself, on the other hand, apart from being a full-time outlaw, could safely claim that in all the hold-ups I'd been involved in, no one had been hurt . . . until now.

It wasn't that I hadn't killed before, I just preferred not to. But if pushed, this six-foot-four giant wouldn't hesitate.

The guard writhed in pain on the ground. I stepped forward and kicked his shotgun out of reach. Then I looked down into the pain-filled face and said caustically, 'You dumb son of a bitch. You just ruined my record.'

'You're an animal,' snapped a young lady in a blue dress. 'A filthy, law-breaking animal.'

'Easy, ma'am,' cautioned the middle-aged stage driver. 'Don't go giving him no excuse to plug another of us.'

The young lady nodded abruptly, her long, black hair bouncing as she did so. 'You're right. He would be just the low-down type of scum that would do so.'

The stage driver flinched at her words.

'I think the young lady needs a good spanking,' Blaze proposed.

'You wouldn't dare,' she said indignantly.

Blaze took a step forward and she yelped and retreated briskly, ducking behind the only other passenger on the stage: a young man with red hair dressed in a gray suit.

'Enough,' I snapped. 'Get the strongbox.'

'We ain't carrying one,' the driver stated calmly.

'You'll get yours, you son of a bitch,' the guard grated from his prone position on the dusty and uneven ground.

I nodded then said, 'Kill the guard.'

'Wait!' it was the young lady who gave the startled cry as she poked her head out from behind her cover. 'It's under the seat of the stage. Inside.'

The stage driver gave a muffled curse.

'Did you want him to kill your friend?' she snapped.

'Hell, no. What kind of feller do you think I am? He was bluffing, miss. He weren't going to shoot. I could see it in his eyes.'

'I guess we'll never know,' I said, and signaled to Miller. 'Find it and get the damned thing open.'

A few moments later, Miller dropped the heavy box onto the trail. Then he took out his Remington six-gun and shot the lock off it. I flipped the lid open and studied the contents.

'Fill the saddle-bags and let's get the hell outta here,' I ordered. Turning my gaze on the driver, I said,

'Get your man into the coach. Get the dude to help you.'

Once it was done, Madden looked at the young lady. 'You might want to take care of him, ma'am. Seems to me a pretty, young lady like yourself might brighten his day some. Better than a bullet anyhow.'

Blaze stepped up beside me and said softly, 'We're done.'

'Good, let's go.'

Late in the afternoon, ten minutes after the stage hit the town of Dry Rock, New Mexico, a large posse thundered out after the outlaws who'd held up the stage. The young lady entered the lobby of the Daybreak Hotel in search of a room.

The clerk looked at the register and passed her a room key.

'There you go, Miss Blake,' he smiled. 'You're in room eight. It's at the top of the stairs and along the hall to your right.'

Meredith Blake returned his smile with a warm one of her own. 'Thank you, kind sir.'

If the man had blushed any harder his spectacles would have fogged up from the heat. Her blue eyes sparkled, causing him to open and close his mouth in stunned silence.

She turned away from the hardwood counter and made her way towards the stairs. Behind her, the clerk watched the sway of her hips as she moved, not once considering that it was strange to have a woman travelling with no luggage.

10

THE OTHER MADDEN

*

On her return from dinner at a local café, Meredith knew there was something wrong the moment she entered her darkened room. She reached inside her small purse and wrapped her hand around a small .44 caliber derringer.

'I been called a lot of things before, but low-down scum is a first,' I said from a black corner of the room.

'I don't know,' Meredith said coolly. 'I kind of thought it suited.'

'Close the door and I'll show you how bad I can be,' I told her.

'Why, Mister Madden, you sir, are a true beast,' Meredith said in her best southern accent.

Once Meredith closed the door, she lit the lamp beside the iron-framed bed. It was only a small room, but was tidy and had what she needed.

'Did you have any problem with the law?' I inquired.

Meredith dropped her purse on the bed and walked towards me. I opened my arms and she slid into them, pressing her body against mine. 'Not one,' she said, and pressed her lips firmly against mine.

I'd met Meredith three years before in Tipton, a small town in Kansas. She had been playing cards with a couple of professional gamblers and was holding her own, right up until the moment that she got caught with a pair of aces up her sleeve.

11

In a blaze of gunfire and smoking guns, I got her out of there, and we've been together ever since. As for what I was doing there in town, I was casing a bank for a job we had planned. Needless to say that we never robbed that one.

She'd been twenty-three at the time and was the female version of a tumbleweed.

When we broke apart, I was, as usual, breathless. She never failed to do it to me. She giggled and asked, 'How much did we get?'

'Your information was good,' I told her. 'There was a touch over five thousand in there.'

The excitement in her voice was evident when she next spoke. 'Where to now, Trace? Where are we going? Do we have enough?'

'Just hold on there, sweet cheeks,' I said, trying to quell her enthusiasm. 'We don't have enough yet.'

The glee on her face was instantly replaced by disappointment. I kissed her softly and said, 'One more job, Mer, one more job.'

Her anger flared and there were sparks in her eyes. 'But that's what you said this time.'

'I promise, Mer, just one more job and then we can go. Leave all of this behind.'

'I don't want to end up in Mexico, Trace,' she snapped at me.

'I told you, Mer, I'm going to take you to California.'

She pouted at me and then said, 'Well, OK then.'

I could understand her frustration. I'd been promising her for an age that we'd get out of the outlaw business. The problem was that we still didn't have enough money for a fresh start. But how much was enough? Despite the rumors, being an outlaw wasn't all it was made out to be. Hell, I'd been an outlaw for over five years. Not by choice I might say, and I'd never scraped together a fortune. Living rough, getting shot at, constantly looking over your shoulder. . . . It sure was a great life. At least now I had a reason to get out of it and hopefully go somewhere far away where the wanted dodgers wouldn't follow.

'Come here,' I said to her, and as Meredith slid into my arms, I was oblivious to the sudden and dramatic turn that our lives were about to take.

Two hundred miles to the north of Dry Rock, in a broad valley in Colorado, Joe Madden stared down from atop a hill at the men erecting a barbed wire fence. Normally that wouldn't worry him, but this one could cost him and two other ranchers everything.

Joe was in his early thirties and had dark hair. He was solidly built, but unlike his brother, he was only five feet ten inches tall.

Trace, he thought. What he'd give to have his wild, younger brother with him now.

The fence being erected by the four men effectively cut him and the two other ranchers off from the only water source that never ran dry. And once summer hit, they were sure to need it. In a long-standing agreement between all the ranchers who

13

shared it, they classed the land as open range and could all access it.

But now it looked as though the fourth rancher, Bren Deavers from the Broken D, was about to renege on the deal, effectively putting a stop to it to claim the water for himself. He was fencing off the whole spring.

Damn it, you can't do that, Joe seethed inwardly. It was all the ranchers' water. Their boundaries converged on that point. Without the water, they couldn't get through summer. The other water sources would dry up and the cattle would die of thirst.

Son of a bitch. You ain't getting away with this.

The bay horse moved beneath Joe as he drew the Winchester rifle from the saddle scabbard and rode down the hill toward the working men.

Emily Madden saw her brother's bay galloping toward the ranch house against a backdrop of granite-peaked mountains and foothills covered in tall trees. It approached at a hard run across the lush green meadow. The only problem was there was no one in the saddle.

Immediately, Emily placed a hand on her chest as alarm flooded her body. Her brown eyes showed all the concern of someone thinking the worst. She pulled her pale head scarf down, letting her brown hair fall to her shoulders while she wiped her hands on the soft fabric.

'Ma! Ruby!'

14

The basket of eggs she'd been carrying was set down on the hard-packed earth of the ranch yard as Emily stepped forward a few paces.

Again, she shouted. 'Ma! Ruby!'

Emily was the youngest of the three Madden children at twenty-three, with a lithe figure and wavy hair.

'What's all the racket about, girl?' Elmira Madden asked, as she banged out through the front door of the ranch house.

'Something has happened to Joe. His horse is coming in.'

Concern etched itself in the deeply lined face of Elmira Madden. 'Oh, Lord.'

'What about Joe?' Ruby Madden asked as she, too, emerged from the ranch house. Her and Joe had been married for the past three years and had a two-year old boy, Jordan.

Hearing the commotion, Bert Frawley came out of the large barn, a pitchfork in his hand. 'What's all the noise?'

Frawley was the only hand employed by the Crooked M, unless there was a lot of work on.

'It's Joe,' Emily told him. 'Something has happened to Joe.'

As the bay drew closer, Emily could see something bobbling along behind the animal. She frowned, not able to make out what it was.

Then, as the lathered mount galloped into the ranch yard, the thing being dragged broke free, and rolled slowly to a stop.

Bert rushed into the yard, waving his arms about to bring the skittish mount to a halt. The scared animal reared up, and when its forelegs hit the earth Bert's hand grabbed the reins.

Meanwhile, Emily's eyes were transfixed on the thing laying in the ranch yard. She took a tentative step forward, followed by another. A fearful lump swelled up in her throat making it almost impossible to swallow.

After another three steps, she was close enough to make out what it was and she recoiled in horror. Wrapped in multiple loops of barbed wire was the battered body of her brother, Joe.

'I can't believe you would even suggest such a thing!' Elmira Madden exploded at her daughter. 'On the day we buried your brother and all.'

'Don't you want to get justice for Joe, Ma?' Emily shot back.

'Justice is for the law to hand out, girl,' Elmira reminded her sternly. 'Not some two-bit outlaw.'

'He's your son,' Emily said.

'Not anymore he ain't.'

'Damn it, Ma,' Emily snapped in frustration.

'Don't you go cussing like that, young lady,' Elmira scolded.

They were about to continue when the ranch house door slammed, signaling the entrance of Bert.

'Damn it, Bert,' Emily said exasperatedly. 'You tell her.'

'Tell her what?'

'Tell her we need Trace,' Emily said.

'Whoa, girl. I ain't so sure Trace showing up around here is a good idea at all.'

'You said yourself that if we don't get access to the water before the end of summer, the cattle will die,' Emily pointed out. 'Now that Deavers has gone and hired himself gunhands to protect it, what do you propose we should do? At least Trace would have an idea.'

'Leave it to the law, girl,' Bert advised her.

'What? You and I both know that the law in Blackmere is bought and paid for by Bren Deavers,' she snorted sarcastically.

'The other ranchers won't stand for it,' Elmira snapped. 'Now leave well enough alone.'

Emily opened her mouth to protest but a withering look from her mother forced her mouth shut. Then Emily looked at Ruby and saw the tears in her eyes. She immediately felt a strong pang of guilt. Her mother was right. Here they were arguing, and they'd only just buried her brother.

But it was far from over.

CHAPTER 2

In between jobs we always holed up at a trading post in the middle of nowhere, run by a German man named Klaus. He was short and bald and a genuinely happy kind of feller. If you crossed him though, he was more than capable of killing you before you even knew about it. So, after the stage job, this was where we headed to plan for the next one.

It was a tidy setup with supplies freighted in monthly to cater for the many travellers that passed through. The building itself was set back from a shallow creek, while behind it was a large stand of rocks surrounded by trees. In behind there, out of sight of prying eyes, was a log cabin that we called home. Cramped as it was, we always seemed to manage.

I was sitting outside, enjoying the morning sun while cleaning my Colt .45, when Blaze came up to me.

'Have you given any more thought about the next job we're going to do?' he asked.

'Gold shipment,' I grunted without looking up.

'Whose?' Blaze asked tentatively, knowing what I was about to say.

'Foster Mining Company.'

'Are you crazy?'

I looked up from what I was doing. 'If we get a shipment from them, then we'll have enough.'

'Enough for what?' he asked me.

'To get out of this life for good,' I said.

'You can't get out of anything if you're dead, Trace,' Blaze pointed out.

I could understand his apprehension. Abraham Foster owned the biggest gold mines in New Mexico, and was the meanest, most crooked son of a bitch you were ever likely to meet. He had forged his empire on the blood of others. His mines had all been acquired by unlawful means. Why do the hard work yourself when others could do it for you?

At the lands office, there was an inside man on his payroll, who notified the magnate when new claims were filed. Foster then watched and waited until the mines started to pay and then he moved in and took over.

'I'm willing to chance it,' I told him.

'How do you think we can get away with it?' Blaze asked.

'We hit one of his transports,' I said.

'You're crazy,' he blurted out. 'Those things have armed guards riding with them.'

'I know.'

'You do realize that if we go ahead and do this,

19

someone is likely to get killed?'

'I ain't got no problem with killing killers,' I said.

'What if it ain't one of them?'

I nodded, my face taking on a grim expression. 'I had thought of that.'

'And what about Meredith?'

'She can't come,' I said with finality. 'Not on this one.'

'And just how do you propose to tell her that?' he asked.

Meredith appeared in the doorway dressed in jeans and a shirt that was tucked in, accentuating her flawless curves. Her long hair was pulled back from her face.

'Tell her what?' she asked.

Let's just say that when I told Meredith what I was proposing, it didn't go well. First, she was perplexed at such an idea. Then she became downright mean when I told her she couldn't come.

'The hell I'm staying behind, Trace Madden,' she fumed. 'I'm coming with you. There ain't no two ways about it.'

'It's too dangerous, Mer,' I stated for the fifth time.

The others emerged from inside the cabin and stood watching. It was Miller who grew brave enough to ask what was actually happening.

Meredith whirled about and with eyes sparkling with rage, snarled, 'This big, dumb son of a bitch has got it into his head that he wants to hit a Foster gold shipment.'

Miller shook his head. 'Not a smart move, Trace. I agree with Mer.'

'Shut up, Miller,' I snapped. 'She don't need any encouragement from you.'

'And he wants to leave me behind while you do it.'

'It's too dangerous for you,' I said in exasperation.

'He's right there, Mer,' Frenchy put in.

'You shut up too,' she snarled.

Suddenly, she whirled around and stormed inside the cabin. Once she was out of sight I looked at the others. The glee etched on their faces said it all. It didn't last long, however. Especially when Meredith returned to our small group, holding a Winchester in her hands.

'You son of a bitch, I should just shoot you now,' she seethed.

The others started to scramble for cover. They'd seen this happen once before and I had the bark off my hide to prove it. Known for her small, but wild fits of jealousy, Meredith had caught me in the arms of another girl in a town over in Arizona. I tried to tell her that she was the bank manager's daughter and that I was gaining information, but she wouldn't hear it. It ended in gunfire and me with a bullet crease in my hindquarters as I was running away.

'Am I interrupting something?' a new voice asked, out of the blue.

We all turned to see Klaus standing there. He, too, had a smirk on his face.

'Just wait while I shoot Trace and we'll be done,' Meredith snapped.

21

'I would, but it is Trace I have come to see,' Klaus said to Mer. 'I have a letter for him.'

I looked at Meredith and asked, 'Do you mind if I read it first? I ain't going anywhere.'

'Oh, damn it,' Meredith cursed. 'Go ahead. I can wait.'

I took the letter from Klaus. The date on it told me it had been posted a week beforehand.

'What I want to know,' Blaze said while I opened the envelope, 'is who knows where you are to send a letter to? And why?'

As I read the letter, the expression on my face changed, prompting Meredith to ask, 'What is it, Trace?'

A ripping pain seemed to tear through my chest as I read it again to make sure that I hadn't misread what was written there. Meredith came forward and stood before me, asking again, this time in a softer tone, 'Trace, what is it?'

I looked into those beautiful blue eyes of hers and was glad she was there. Inside, a mix of sadness and anger threatened to consume me.

'It's my brother,' I managed to get out. 'He's dead. Someone killed him.'

Half an hour later we all sat around the table inside the dimly lit cabin.

'What do you want to do?' Blaze asked me.

'My sister says they need help,' I told them all. 'If they don't get it, then all their stock will die.'

'Nasty way to go,' Frenchy said in disgust. 'Bob

wire, dragging.'

'What about the law?' Meredith asked me.

'No surprise there; it's as crooked as a dog's hind leg, so that ain't a problem,' I informed her.

'It sounds as though you've made up your mind to go,' Blaze said.

'They need my help,' I pointed out.

'So when are you leaving?' Miller asked.

'After the next job,' I told them.

'Damn it, Trace,' Meredith exploded.

'Wait, Mer, let me explain,' I said, holding up a hand.

'OK, but I still won't like it.'

'The next shipment is a couple of days away. We take it and then we have enough to get to California. Blaze and the others hang on to it until we get back here to divvy up. Which will be after the trouble with my family is fixed.'

My gaze settled on Blaze. 'You OK with that?'

'Sure.'

'Does that mean I'm going with you?' Meredith asked me hopefully.

'No.'

'Trace. . . .'

'Hold on, I want you to do something else for me.'

'Trace,' Blaze said, interrupting. 'Why don't we leave it until you get done with your business?'

'I'm for that,' put in Frenchy.

'It means that Mer can go with you, Trace,' Blaze pointed out. 'Saves her shooting you.'

I thought long about it before agreeing and

23

nodded my consent. 'OK then. We'll do it that way.'

Two days later, while Meredith and I were travelling north, Blaze and the others pulled a job of their own with what would turn out to be disastrous consequences.

CHAPTER 3

I stared down at my brother's grave in silence. Beside me, Meredith had her arm hooked through mine. On the grave was a plain white marker with the words Joe Madden painted in black. Overhead, the sky was leaden gray and there was a chill in the air as the last vestiges of winter refused to let go.

The cemetery sat on a low hill on the outskirts of Blackmere, surrounded by a grove of trees.

In the week that had passed since we'd left the cabin, I'd let my beard grow over my square-jawed face. It paid to be careful in my line of work. I let my right hand drift casually down to the holstered Colt. Meredith sensed that something was wrong and turned her gaze to stare at me inquisitively.

'Strangers in town?' the voice behind us asked.

We turned around to see three men standing no more than fifteen feet away.

'Sorry?' I said.

The wiry-looking man in the middle repeated his words. 'Strangers in town?'

Before answering I ran a wary gaze over the two
men with him. One was thinly built like the speaker
and had black hair tucked away under a brown hat.
The other was larger, rounder, and I guessed there to
be a fair amount of power in his six-foot-two frame.

I said, 'Who's asking?'

The wiry man drew back the flap of his black coat
and showed a sheriff's badge.

'Sheriff Herman Brody,' he informed me. 'These
other two are my deputies, Pert and Cal.'

I felt Meredith tense beside me, her fingers
digging into my arm.

Nodding, I said, 'Uh-huh.'

'I didn't catch your name,' Brody pressed.

'I didn't give it.'

Brody eyed me warily. 'Did you know him?'

'Who?'

'The feller in the grave.'

I nodded. 'A long time ago. I worked on his ranch
for a while when I was a young 'un. Heard he died
and thought I would come and pay my respects.
Guess I was too late.'

'Only by a couple of weeks,' the one named Cal
snorted.

I stared hard at him and he shuffled uncomfort-
ably.

'Come now, Cal,' the sheriff admonished his
deputy. 'The man's probably come a long way to see
his friend buried right. Show a little respect.'

'What about you, missy?' Brody asked, turning his
attention to Meredith. 'Did you know the deceased?'

She shook her head. 'No.'

'Do you people plan on staying long?'

'Just until we see the family and then we'll be going home,' I lied.

'Oh, where's that?' Brody asked.

'New Mexico.'

Brody gave me a blank stare.

'Is there anything else?' I inquired.

'There's something about you, stranger,' he said finally. 'I can't put my finger on it yet, but I'm certain there's something that don't set right.'

'Come and find me when you work it out,' I told him and then Meredith and I stepped around the three men and began to walk over to the tree where our horses were tied.

Behind me I heard one of them say, 'You didn't get their names, Brody. Mr Deavers ain't going to like that. He said from now on we are to get the names of any strangers who come to town.'

'I know, damn it,' Brody snapped. 'Shut up.'

Then it happened. We hadn't quite reached our horses when the deputy known as Pert blurted out, 'Shceiit, I know. '

That was all he said before I'd palmed up my Colt, cocked it, and turned, bringing it to bear. It all happened so fast not one of them had time to react. Even Pert, who'd recognized me, only had his gun half drawn.

'What the hell, stranger?' Brody gasped.

'Let go of the six-gun, Pert,' I ordered. 'Mer, get the horses ready.'

'Who are you?' Brody hissed.

It was Pert who told him. 'He's Trace Madden, Brody. He's the outlaw brother.'

'Well, I'll be . . .' the Blackmere sheriff said, bewildered.

'Now that you know who I am,' I told him, 'I'll answer your question. I'm staying around until I find out who killed my brother.'

'Take my advice, Madden,' Brody warned me. 'People around here don't cotton to outlaws. Might pay for you to ride on before you get locked away. Or worse.'

I smiled mirthlessly. 'Maybe you should take your own advice.'

'Are you ready, Trace?' Meredith called out to me.

'Almost,' I called over my shoulder. 'You fellers unhitch them gun-belts. I ain't about to leave you armed while my back is turned to you.'

They did as they were ordered, without fuss or protest. Once they'd finished I told them to take a couple of steps back, after which I grabbed up their guns and tossed them as far as I could.

'Stay the hell outta Blackmere, Madden,' Brody snapped at me. 'If I find you there, we won't lock you in jail. We'll kill you.'

I nodded. 'I'll keep that in mind. Mer, keep an eye on them while I get mounted.'

Meredith drew a Winchester '76 from the saddle scabbard of the horse she rode. I smiled as I heard her work the lever with ease.

'Don't make no foolish moves,' I warned them.

'She knows how to shoot.'

A few moments later I was mounted and we were riding away from Blackmere.

'Where are we headed now?' Meredith asked me over the top of thundering hoofs.

'The Crooked M.'

The trail to the ranch topped a low ridge that afforded a view of the stunning valley, and there before us was the Crooked M.

'It sure is beautiful country,' Meredith commented, looking at the scene before her.

'You should see it in the fall,' I said, remembering the myriad oranges, golds and reds the leaves on the trees used to turn at that time of year. 'It's something special, that's for sure.'

'I can see why your family like it here,' she said.

We eased the horses forward down the sloping trail, and half a mile further on rode into the ranch yard. The place hadn't changed much in the time since I'd left. The barn looked a little rundown, the ranch house had a new veranda and the corral had new lodge pole rails in it.

I was suddenly taken aback when I saw the large pine tree with a homemade swing strung from a low branch. There was only one reason why there would be a swing there. A child. And I knew Emily wasn't married, so that left Joe. Joe had a kid, and now he was dead.

Right then and there my resolve hardened to get to the bottom of what had happened to my brother.

'Can I help you two people?' a gravelly voice asked.

I hipped in the saddle and saw Bert coming from behind the bunkhouse. He looked a little more worn than when I'd last seen him, but it was him all right.

'Hello, Bert,' I greeted him.

'Glory be,' he managed to get out, stunned. 'Is that you, Trace?'

'Yeah, it's me,' I confirmed.

'Damn, boy. You shouldn't be here. Not now.'

'Why, Bert?'

'Did Emily send for you?'

I nodded.

'Yeah, she would. Even after her ma told her not to.' His eyes travelled to Meredith. 'Who's your friend?'

'My name is Meredith.'

'Are you an outlaw too?'

'Kind of nosey, ain't you?' Meredith shot back.

Bert gave her a wry smile. 'You got spunk as well as looks. You got yourself a keeper there, Trace.'

I looked at Meredith and said, 'Yes, I do.'

The door to the ranch house opened and Emily appeared. 'Trace? Is that you? It is you!'

Emily launched herself from the veranda and out into the yard, running toward me. I slid from the saddle in time to wrap her up in my arms.

'Look at you, little sis, all grown up.'

'It's so good to see you,' she said, planting a big kiss on my bearded cheek. 'I wasn't sure you would come.'

'He came and now he can get the hell off my land.'

I looked over at the veranda and saw her standing there; looking a little older, grayer, face lined.

'Hi, Ma,' I said. 'It's been a while.'

'Not long enough,' she said harshly. 'Get back on that horse of yours and get off my land. And take your hussy with you.'

'Ma!' Emily exclaimed. 'You can't do that.'

I winced at her words. Not because they were harsh, but because I knew what would come next.

'Listen up, old woman,' Meredith snapped loudly. 'I may be a lot of things, but a hussy ain't one of them. And if you weren't Trace's ma, I'd climb down and bust you in the kisser.'

Just as I thought. You'd get the same result by slapping a grizzly on the ass.

What happened next was unexpected. Instead of firing back with a burr under her saddle, Ma nodded abruptly and said, 'Get down off your horse and come inside.'

There was a brief period of stunned silence before Meredith climbed down and started to walk towards the ranch house. As she stepped up onto the veranda, Ma looked at me and said sternly, 'You stay out here.'

I watched as they disappeared inside and then turned to face Emily and Bert and said, 'Tell me what's going on.'

'Bren Deavers put bob wire around the spring to stop the other ranchers getting at it,' Bert said. 'I think Joe found them doing it and they wrapped him in the stuff and tied it to his horse. They scared the animal and it dragged him home. There was no way he could survive a dragging that far.'

'I ain't heard of this Deavers feller. Who is he? What did he say?' I asked.

'Deavers turned up two years ago and bought the Taylor spread. Up until now, he's been fine, but things have changed. He says the spring is on his land and he has every right to fence it,' Bert said, answering my questions. 'He had it certified by the lands office and has the map and papers to prove it. As for Joe, Deavers said that he must've been trying to pull the fence down and got tangled up in the wire.'

'And he has the law on his side,' I added. 'I ran into the sheriff and his deputies at the cemetery.'

'Did they recognize you?' Emily asked hurriedly.

I nodded. 'They did, but don't worry, I can handle them.'

I looked over at the house again for the third or fourth time.

'Are you worried about what Ma is saying in there?' Emily asked.

I shook my head. 'I'm worried about what Meredith is saying.'

'She seems nice enough,' Emily commented.

I nodded. 'Tell me about Joe's family.'

'Ruby and Jordy are in town,' she said, watching my eyes.

'Why?'

32

'Ruby is having trouble with the fact that Joe is gone. She keeps seeing him wrapped in that ghastly stuff in the middle of the yard.'

'Yeah, can't have been good.'

'What do you plan on doing now you're back, Trace?' Bert asked.

I stared at him and there was a hard edge to my voice when I spoke. 'I'm going to find the bastard who killed Joe.'

CHAPTER 4

The look of concern on Bren Deavers' face said it all.
Things seemed to have settled after the death of Joe
Madden and he continued to plan. Once the
summer had finished he would have the other three
ranches and be able to get down to making real
money – and lots of it.

Then Brody turned up that afternoon with the
news that Trace Madden had come back to
Blackmere with the intention of finding out what
had happened to his brother.

'I guess he'll have to go, the same as his brother,'
Rance Caldwell surmised when Brody finished speak-
ing.

The rancher stood up from his position on the
leather lounge. He walked across to a large mul-
lioned window of his study and looked out across the
dry, hard-packed earth of the ranch yard and
beyond. He took a sip from the glass of whiskey he
held and then turned around.

Deavers was a large, solidly-built man in his early
forties. He had salt-and-pepper hair and a face that
was starting to show the lines that came with age. He

was also a man who was used to getting what he wanted and didn't suffer fools.

'You said he has a woman with him?' Deavers asked.

'Yeah.'

Deavers growled. 'Arrest the son of a bitch and lock him up.'

'It ain't going to be that simple, Bren. He's a different beast compared to the others. He'll fight hard.'

'I don't care; he's an outlaw. Lock . . . him . . . up.'

'I'll do what I can.'

'You'll do better.'

'Sure.'

After he was gone, Caldwell asked, 'What are you thinking?'

'That I want Madden out of the way.'

When the four men walked into the dim trading post, Klaus knew that all his nightmares had finally come true. Under his breath he murmured, '*Mein Gott. Es sind die vier Reiter!*' 'My God. It is the four horsemen!'

'What's the matter, friend?' Cleve Hardin asked. 'You look like you've seen a ghost.'

'*Ja.*' Klaus corrected himself. 'Yes, what is it you want?'

'Straight to the point; I like that,' Cleve acknowledged. 'Me and my friends here are looking for some fellers and thought maybe you might know them.'

Klaus ran his gaze over the four men nervously.

Their clothing made them look like drifters, down-and-out cowhands moving from one job to the next. They could be outlaws, but if so, they would just kill him and take what they wanted.

It was their faces. All were unshaven; a couple had obvious scars. There was something about their eyes, cruel and dark. A shiver ran through Klaus' body.

'He looks like he's about to piss himself, Cleve,' one of the men said.

'I agree, Drake,' the man named Cleve said. 'I agree. You know what that tells me?'

'What?'

'It tells me that he knows exactly why we're here.'

Panic filled Klaus' eyes as two of the men stepped forward. He scrambled for the shotgun under the counter but was painfully slow. As he brought it up, a six-gun rapped sharply across the side of his head.

Klaus staggered and dropped the cut-down shotgun. He held a hand to his head, and when it came away it was red.

Cleve stepped forward and grabbed the still stunned Klaus by the shirt collar. He said, 'Now, let's try again.'

'How's the shoulder, Frenchy?' Blaze asked the wounded outlaw as he stepped outside the cabin and into the sunlight.

'It's all right, Blaze, no thanks to you,' he growled, moving it around. 'It's starting to free up a little.'

'Are you still mad at me?' Blaze asked.

'Damn right, Blaze. We told Trace we weren't

36

going to do anything but wait for him to get back, and then we ride off and try robbing a bank that Cleve Hardin is already in the process of doing over. I get shot and Hardin and his men get arrested.'

'It all worked out. We got the money.'

'Only because one of Hardin's men dropped it.'

Frenchy stepped out beyond where Blaze was enjoying the sun, sitting on an old stump. The wounded outlaw then turned around and looked at Blaze. His expression had changed, and Blaze frowned at him.

'What's up, Frenchy?' he asked.

'There's someone in the trees,' he said, trying not to panic and warn the intruders. 'I'm thinking we may have. . . .'

That was as far as Frenchy got before his chest seemed to explode as a bullet ripped through his torso from the back, the report of a gunshot hot on its heels. His mouth flew wide from the shock of the blow. He staggered forward a few steps before he began to sag.

Blaze reached out and grabbed the mortally wounded outlaw by the shirt and held him erect. Then he tried to make himself as small as possible while using all his strength to walk backwards, using his dead friend for a shield.

Frenchy's body shuddered under the impact of more bullets. Realizing that what he was trying to do wasn't going to work for long, Blaze let him go and ran for the door behind him.

He crashed through the opening and landed on

the floor as a hail of lead followed him through. Breathing hard, Blaze scrambled to the left where the log walls offered more protection.

'What the hell is going on?' Miller screeched. 'Where's Frenchy?'

Blaze looked across at the outlaw who cowered beneath the table.

'He's dead!' Blaze shouted. 'Just like we will be if we don't get outta here. Can you get to the rifles?'

'I'll try.'

There was a brief lull in the shooting and Miller grabbed up both the rifles from where they leaned against the rough wall. He tossed one to Blaze and kept the other for himself.

'Get out the back and organize the horses,' Blaze ordered him. 'I'll try and keep them busy while you do it.'

'Keep who busy, Blaze?' Miller asked, bewildered.

'I ain't sure, but I got me a feeling.'

'Hey, you in the cabin. You there, Blaze? I've come for my money.'

'That's Cleve Hardin,' Miller about exploded.

'Go get the damned horses ready.'

Miller slipped out the back while Blaze moved across to the window. More bullets peppered the building. Blaze stuck the Winchester's barrel out the window and fired off three fast shots.

Immediately it drew a response as lead hammered into the timber surrounding the window frame. Blaze let rip another volley of four shots before he backed away from the window. He then turned and hurried to the door that Miller had slipped out.

He found Miller just cinching the last saddle. 'That was damn quick.'

'What do you expect? We're getting shot at.'

'Yeah, let's get the hell out of here before they realize something's wrong.'

'Where we going, Blaze?'

'To find Trace. Get mounted.'

By the time the attackers realized all was not right, they were gone.

It was Meredith who woke me the following morning. That was after the rooster had done so before the sun was even up. I contemplated shooting it for a time as it crowed incessantly, but just as I stood up from my hay mattress with Colt in hand, it stopped.

'Morning, handsome,' she greeted cheerily and planted a kiss on my lips. 'How did you sleep?'

Sleep I could have done with more of. The kiss . . . I reached out and dragged her down on top of me and planted one of my own on her full lips.

'I slept like a baby,' I lied when she pushed back from me. But she knew that.

'Liar,' she said. 'You know I can tell when you're not telling me the truth.'

'How did you sleep in there with the she bear?' I asked, changing the subject.

Meredith punched me hard on my left arm. 'Your *mother* is quite nice when you get to know her.'

'She eats her young, you know?' I said with a wry smile. 'There used to be six of us.'

'Trace Madden, you take that back,' Meredith said indignantly. 'That woman cares for you more than you'll ever know.'

I looked around the barn. 'She sure has a funny way of showing it.'

Meredith smiled at me. I never got used to seeing the way her eyes lit up when she did.

'Why are you in the barn, anyway?' she asked me. 'What was wrong with the bunkhouse?'

'Bert was afraid Ma might get all ornery with him if I did, so I told him I'd sleep out here.'

'He was right, I would've done just that,' Ma said sternly from the doorway of the barn.

Meredith turned red and rolled off me. Ma stood there framed by the morning sunlight, wearing a gray dress and white apron.

'Come on in, Ma,' I told her. 'It's your barn after all.'

She took two steps and stopped.

Meredith stood up and brushed strands of hay from her clothes. 'I'll go and chop firewood.'

I looked at her and raised an eyebrow. She in return mouthed something I couldn't quite make out and then left us alone.

'She's a good woman, that one,' Ma said to me, breaking the tense silence.

I nodded. 'She is.'

'Too good for the likes of you, Trace Madden,' she snapped. 'You ought not be dragging her around with your outlaw ways.'

I remained silent. What could I say? She was right.

'I have to go to town this morning and get a few things,' she said to me. 'And to see Ruby and Jordy.'

'I'll come with you,' I told her.

Ma's eyes grew hard and she snapped, 'No, you won't. I don't want you going anywhere near them. Understand? Especially Jordy. I don't want him hanging around no common outlaw.'

Her words bit deep, but I didn't let it show. 'I have no intention of seeing them. I want to have another word with the sheriff about Joe.'

A dark shadow overcame Ma's face and she said through gritted teeth, 'That no account. All he is, is a hired gun for Bren Deavers. Even if he found out who it was killed Joe, he wouldn't do anything about it.'

'I still aim to have a talk to him. I've a hunch he'll know more about it than we do.'

'Fine,' Ma snapped again. 'But you stay away from your brother's wife and boy, like I said.'

I nodded. 'All right, Ma.'

Nodding abruptly, she turned away and started walking out the double-doors. I called after her, 'It's good to see you, Ma.'

She stopped, and I noticed her stiffen slightly. 'Your sister and I'll be leaving inside the hour.'

'I'll be ready,' I told her and then she kept walking.

No sooner had she left than Meredith appeared in the doorway. Giving me her best winning smile, she asked, 'Are we going to town?'

'You know we are,' I said. 'You were outside listening all the time.'

She feigned a look of innocence and said, 'Who, me?'

I just shook my head and said to her, 'Put your best dress on, Mer. We'll be leaving soon.'

'I can't wear my gun if I have a dress on,' she snapped.

'Exactly.'

CHAPTER 5

Ma, Emily, and Meredith rode in the wagon, which Bert drove. Ma sat beside Bert on the seat while my sister and Mer sat in the back. The looks she was giving me every time they hit a bump told me that sooner or later I was going to get an ear bashing.

I'd deal with it when it happened. I guess my smiles didn't help the matter much, but in its own special way it was funny.

Blackmere hadn't changed much since I'd left all those years ago. The Palace Saloon had some competition now from a place across the street called The Red Queen. The blacksmith, drygoods store, lands office, saddlers, and livery were still the same. Even the doctor's shingle outside a small, white-washed cottage had the same name on it.

'I thought Doc Grace would've been dead by now,' I said to Ma as we continued along the street and past his place. 'He was about there when I left.'

'He's too ornery to die,' Ma said curtly and then went back to her silence.

43

The further we traveled along the black-dirt street, the more on edge I became, until it came to a point where I flipped the hammer-thong off my Colt and rested my hand on its butt.

Meredith caught me doing it and frowned. I gave her a reassuring smile and returned my gaze to the direction we were going. All the while I couldn't help but think that we were riding into the jaws of the beast.

'He's here,' Pert said excitedly as he barged into the jail through the open door.

Brody swung his feet down off the scarred desktop and looked questioningly at his deputy. 'Who's here?'

'Trace Madden,' Pert blurted out. 'Him and his family just came in. I saw them coming along the street. They stopped near Hopper's place.'

'Must be getting some supplies,' Brody surmised.

'What are we going to do?' Pert asked the sheriff.

'What do you mean?'

'Didn't Mr Deavers want us to arrest him?'

'Yeah, he did,' Brody allowed.

'Are we going to do it then?'

Brody nodded. 'Go and get Cal. I'll meet you over at Hopper's store.'

Pert nodded eagerly and disappeared out the door, while Brody walked across to the gunrack that hung on the back wall of the dimly lit jail. He took down a '76 Winchester and checked to see that it was loaded before he, too, walked out onto the street.

*

Doug Hopper shook noticeably as he handed Ma the packet of buttons she'd just bought. I guess having a wanted fugitive in his store didn't help matters any. Hell, it wasn't like I was there to rob him or anything.

'Mr Hopper,' I said, getting his attention.

He jumped and then looked at me wide-eyed. 'Y-Yes, sir?'

'When you're finished with my Ma, there's a couple of things that I'd like to get.'

He swallowed hard and nodded jerkily. 'No problem, Mr Madden.'

'I ain't no Mister,' I said, trying to ease the tension. 'Just call me Trace.'

He nodded again and finished putting together the rest of Ma's order. Off to one side, Meredith and Emily were looking at bolts of cloth as they tried to work out what would be the best to make a dress out of.

She looked up at me and smiled. It was the happiest I'd seen her in a long while. I think the time with my family was working wonders on her.

Sadly, her happiness was about to be shattered by a reminder of what we really were.

When the three lawmen came in I was out of sight behind one of the store's displays. The only reason I knew something was wrong was because Hopper suddenly paled and Emily looked alarmed.

'Where is your outlaw son?' a voice said. I quickly recognized it as the sheriff, Brody.

Meredith gave me a warning look and I stepped back quickly.

Ma shrugged. 'I wouldn't know. Have you found the killer of my boy yet?'

'You've been told, old woman,' Brody snapped curtly. 'It was found to be an accident. Nothing more.'

Ma snorted. 'An accident, my Aunt Mary's big rump. He was murdered, and you know it. You're just so deep in Deavers' hip pocket, all you can smell is what he spouts from his rear end.'

Yep, you got to hand it to Ma, she sure has a way with words.

'I ain't going to stand here and bandy with you all day, old woman,' Brody growled. 'I came for your son. However, if he ain't here, his whore will do.'

Now that was like throwing kerosene on a fire.

I don't know where she hid it, or even how it appeared so quick, but the Colt in Meredith's hand looked as big as a cannon from where I stood, and I expect that it looked three times that size to Brody.

'Mer, wait,' I snapped loudly.

'I knew you was here!' Brody exclaimed.

'Wait, hell,' she snarled, not taking her eyes from the sheriff and his two deputies. 'The son of a bitch called me a whore.'

'You shoot him, girl,' Ma cackled from where she stood. 'Ain't nothing he deserves more.'

'Not helping, Ma,' I cautioned her.

'Well it's true,' she snapped.

Hopper had disappeared behind his counter to

clear the imminent line of fire.

'Don't do anything foolish, girly,' Brody said with a nervous tone in his voice. 'Killing a law officer will get you hung quick smart.'

'It's a good thing I ain't shooting one then,' Meredith said coldly. 'Polecats, on the other hand, I'll shoot every day if I get the chance.'

I saw one of the deputies grab for his gun. It was fast enough to be slow, so you could imagine his astonishment when he was staring down the barrel of my Peacemaker. His six-gun hadn't even cleared leather.

'Keep on dragging that thing if you want to die of lead poisoning,' I warned him.

His hand opened reflexively as though the walnut grips of his gun butt had scalded him.

I shifted my gaze to Brody. 'Sheriff, if you don't want to die this day, I suggest you apologize to the lady.'

'The hell I will,' he snarled with an indignant look.

I shook my head solemnly. 'I tried.'

The hammer going back on Meredith's Colt seemed loud to me. But to Brody, I swear it must've almost burst his eardrums because he just about threw his arms out of joint as they went up.

'All right, I'm sorry,' he blurted out.

'About what?' Meredith growled.

'For calling . . . you a whore,' Brody stammered.

'Damn it, girl, shoot him anyway,' Ma cried out.

'Shut it, Ma,' I snapped.

'Don't you talk to your ma that way,' she scolded

me, bringing back memories of my childhood.

The situation was about to spiral out of control and the last thing I wanted was a gunfight in these confined conditions.

'Get out of here,' I snapped at Brody. 'If you try something like this again, you'd best come shooting. Tell your boss that, too.'

'Wait!' Meredith said.

'Mer,' I said cautiously, 'let the men go.'

She smiled at me. 'In a minute.'

I hated it when she did that. It meant that things didn't bode well for Brody at all.

A sigh of resignation escaped my lips just before she took a couple of steps forward and launched a right hook that any prizefighter would have been proud of. The crunching sound that her bunched fist made as it flattened Brody's nose made me wince.

When she stepped back, shaking the pain from her hand, it allowed me a better view of the free-flowing blood that had begun to pour from Brody's mangled face.

His hand flew to his nose and came away red. Tears streamed down his cheeks and he said in an accusing voice, 'You bitch, you broke my nose.'

Once again, I had reason to shake my head. Some people never learn. The next place to feel Meredith's wrath was his crotch as she stepped forward and brought up her right leg, her booted foot catching him unaware.

A squeak escaped the sheriff's lips as he buckled at the knees, his eyes bulging, and face almost the color of that which ran from his nose.

I looked at the two deputies and said to them, 'You'd best get your boss out of here before he talks himself into a grave.'

Without hesitation, they picked Brody up from the floor and helped him out of the shop. I looked at Meredith as I put my Colt away and scowled.

'What?' she asked, feigning innocence for the second time that day.

'Damn, girl,' Ma chortled, 'You sure are starting to grow on a person.'

'Don't encourage her, Ma,' I said. 'She don't need it. And where on earth did you pull that damned Colt from?'

Meredith just smiled at me.

Shaking my head for the hundredth time, I looked about the store. 'Mr Hopper? You can come out now. It's all over.'

The storekeeper's head popped up over the countertop, his eyes wide with shock. 'Have they gone?'

'Yes, Mr Hopper, they've gone.'

'If you're all through hiding down there, I'd like the rest of my order now,' Ma chided him.

Hopper nodded, gathering himself. 'Yes, quite; I'll be right with you.'

I felt Meredith beside me as she pressed against my arm. I shifted my gaze and looked into those blue eyes of hers, knowing that my annoyance at what had just happened wouldn't go any further.

'How's your hand?' I asked.

She gave me a sweet smile. 'Hurts.'

'Good.'

She frowned at me. 'What's wrong with you?'

'I didn't bring you here to get shot. Just remember that. Don't go doing anything stupid.'

'Aww. You care.'

'Damn it, Meredith,' I snapped furiously. 'This is serious. These fellers are dangerous. I want you alive, not in a hole in the ground.'

Meredith looked into my eyes and seemed about to say something else but then changed her mind.

'OK, Trace,' she assured me. 'I'll be careful.'

I nodded. 'All right. You and the others wait here.'

'Where are you going?' Ma asked me.

'Outside, Ma.'

'Why can't we come?' she protested to my back. 'We've finished here.'

I ignored her and kept walking toward the door.

'Trace?' she called after me.

I heard Meredith say to her, 'He's going to check outside. I guess he figures the sheriff and his deputies could be waiting for us to come out.'

'Well get out there and help him,' Ma ordered.

'He doesn't need our help,' Meredith told her. 'One thing I know about Trace Madden is that he's quite capable.'

CHAPTER 6

'I'm going to kill that son of a bitch and his whore,' Sheriff Herman Brody snarled, blood-flecked spittle flying from his lips. 'Just see if I don't.'

His deputies stared at him as he wiped the blood from his face with his kerchief. He'd dipped it in one of the troughs that were spaced out along the main street. The front of his shirt was bloodstained, much like large, red rain drops.

'What do you want to do, Brody?' Cal asked his boss. 'Deavers didn't say anything about killing him.'

'Yeah, well. Locked up, dead, it's all the same.'

Pert nodded. 'Dead's better. But I ain't going to kill no woman.'

'You'll do as I tell you,' Brody hissed. 'Now get over the other side of the street and wait.'

Pert did as he was told and sauntered across the street dragging his feet, the heels of his boots leaving scuff marks in the dirt.

Brody then focused on Cal. 'You stay this side and don't do anything until I do. If you've a mind, you can kill that old ranch hand.'

Cal nodded. Unlike Pert, he had no qualms about whom he killed.

'Now all we gotta do is wait,' Brody told him.

And as it turned out, they didn't have long to wait at all.

The moment my boots hit the uneven plank boardwalk, I knew there was something wrong. Some would call it a sixth sense. Me, I called it lack of townsfolk. Quite simply I could see no one.

I used my thumb to flick the hammer-thong off my Peacemaker and walked across the boardwalk, the heels of my boots clunking loudly in the silence that cloaked the town.

I stepped off and out into the street, my eyes darting back and forth taking in all I could. Then I saw them. Spread out, the two deputies on the boardwalks on opposite sides of the street.

I pushed my hat back apiece on my head before I started to walk towards them. Every step I took seemed to jar up my legs.

'Not hiding behind your bitch this time, outlaw?' Brody sneered when I was close enough.

I stopped, staring at him but said nothing. To my left and right his deputies moved to clear their line of fire from the uprights that held up the awnings.

'This is your play, is it?' I asked him. 'Kill the other brother while you can?'

'Deavers didn't say to kill you, Madden; this one's on me,' he gloated. 'Know this: when we've put you

52

down, we'll go after your whore.'

I shook my head at his feeble attempt to get a rise out of me. Trying to throw me off, which meant he was worried.

'There you go again,' I said to him. 'You ought not speak about the woman I love in such a fashion.'

'Yeah? Why not?'

My right arm blurred and the Peacemaker came clear of its holster and roared. Flame belched from its muzzle as the deadly .45 caliber slug ripped through the morning air and punched into the chest of the deputy on the left.

My aim shifted, and I fired again. This time Brody fell back in a tangle of arms and legs. Shifting my aim again, I almost blew the second deputy out of his boots with another well-placed shot.

Bam, bam, bam, and it was all over.

I punched the empty shells from the Peacemaker and replaced them with live rounds. I then turned to see Ma and Emily standing transfixed by the violence they'd witnessed. I thought they'd been inside but apparently they'd followed me out.

Now Ma is a tough woman, but I think the reality that one of her sons could be capable of what she'd witnessed shook her. Sure, she'd been all talk in the store, but now that it had actually happened, it had changed everything. She opened her mouth to say something, but words failed to emerge.

She tried again and this time she said, 'In all my born days, I never would have thought that one of my sons could be so cold with killing.'

My gaze was unwavering when I said, 'If you think that was cold, Ma, just remember this. They would have shot me down and killed any one of you who tried to interfere. As it was, Brody had designs on killing Meredith anyway. If push comes to shove, I'll do it again.'

Ma turned and walked toward the wagon. Emily did the same. Meredith came over to me and took me by the arm.

'Give her time, Trace. That would be a lot for her to take in. One of her sons is dead and the other just shot three men.'

I nodded. 'She can take all the time she needs after this is over. Because from here on, it'll only get worse.'

'Elmira! Emily! Is everything all right?' a woman's frantic voice called out as she hurried across the street.

Meredith and I turned and saw a slim, good-looking woman with long brown hair, wearing a no-frills gray dress.

They talked amongst themselves for a short time and then I saw the woman look in our direction. Even from where we stood I could see her face had paled some.

'Come on,' I said to Meredith and started to walk over to them.

'Don't you come near us,' Ma growled at me when I got close. 'There's nothing for you here.'

'Shut down, Ma,' I said softly, trying not to upset her.

'Don't you talk to your ma like that, Trace Madden,' she scolded.

'Are you Ruby?' I asked the woman.

'No, she ain't, now go away,' Ma snapped.

'It's OK, Elmira,' Ruby said softly and then looked at me. 'Yes, I am.'

'I'm sorry for your loss, ma'am,' I told her. 'I can see Joe was a lucky man.'

'Thank you,' she said with a wan smile.

'This is Meredith,' I said, introducing her. 'She kinda keeps me in line.'

'Doesn't seem to be working out so well, does it?' Ruby observed.

'They were bad men,' I said, offering up a weak defense.

She nodded and then turned back to Ma. 'I must be going. I only wanted to see if you were all right. Maybe you could come by to see Jordy before you leave town?'

I saw Ma's face light up. 'I'll be along directly.'

I watched her walk away and Ma turned to face me. There was something different in her face this time. Something brought on by the mention of Joe's son.

'I want you to stay away from Jordan,' she said to me. It wasn't an order, more a request.

Nodding I said, 'OK, Ma.'

'For the time being,' she said. 'If this gets worse, as you seem to think it will, then I don't want him or her anywhere near it. Can you do that?'

'I can do that.'

'Good. Thank you,' she said, grateful that I didn't argue about it. 'Now, I must go see my grandson.'

People were starting to gather, gawking at the bodies where they lay. Not one person that I saw seemed distressed about the men's passing.

'That was a good thing you did,' Meredith said to me.

'What was?'

'Not putting up a fight about seeing your nephew.'

I shrugged. 'Ma's right. The further they are away from this, the better.'

I gave Bert a hand to load the last of the supplies into the wagon while Meredith and Emily stood to one side talking between themselves.

The bodies were soon taken away, and it was at that point a well-dressed man appeared and made me an offer that he thought I couldn't refuse.

'You're plumb crazy,' I said to the balding man in the immaculate suit. 'Do you know who I am?'

Mayor Joshua Dean looked hurt at first, but he didn't let that sway him from his current mission.

'I do,' he acknowledged.

'You know I'm an outlaw?'

'Yes.'

'And yet you still want me to pin on the sheriff's badge?'

'Yes.'

'No.'

'But why?' he asked in exasperation.

I shook my head in bewilderment. 'You don't need

me. Put a man in charge who's honest. I'm sure you can find one.'

'If we don't find someone soon then Deavers will put someone else in office that will be the same as, or worse than those you killed. If that's even possible.'

'Think about it, Trace,' Emily encouraged me. 'It is a chance to get your life back on track.'

'My life's fine the way it is,' I snapped impatiently.

'Ahem.'

I turned and looked at Meredith. 'Don't you start.'

The clatter of hoofbeats drew our attention as a tall cowboy on a spent-looking sorrel came charging into the main street. He hauled back on the reins so hard that the poor bronc almost sat on its rump. Then he jumped from the saddle and hurried toward our group.

My hand dropped to the Peacemaker at my hip as I waited to see what would happen next.

'Emily!' he cried out. 'Are you OK?'

'Jeff, yes, I'm fine,' Emily assured the newcomer.

'When I heard, I just had to come and see you.'

He wrapped his arms around her and held her tight. I looked at Meredith and she winked at me. I rolled my eyes and said, 'Come on, Mer, let's get outta here before it becomes catching.'

'You'll think about my proposal?' the mayor asked hopefully before I could move.

'Nope.'

'But we need a sheriff,' he persisted.

Before I could open my mouth and vent my displeasure at his unwillingness to give up, Jeff Harper

57

said, 'I'll do it.'

'Jeff, no,' Emily gasped.

'I'd think seriously about what you're proposing, son,' the mayor said.

The young man with the blond hair wouldn't be swayed. 'I can do it. I can't be a cowhand all of my life.'

'You realize that you'll more than likely have to go against Rance Caldwell, don't you?'

I felt Meredith grab my arm. It was a name we both knew. Caldwell was nothing but a hired gun and killer. This young man before us would be in over his head if he pinned on the badge.

'Let it go,' I advised him. 'Caldwell ain't someone you want to mess with.'

His eyes fixed on me. 'Who are you?'

'This is my brother, Trace,' Emily told him.

He eyed me suspiciously. 'The outlaw?'

I nodded. 'Yeah, the outlaw.'

Then the realization hit. 'It was you they said killed these men.'

'Yeah.'

'Jeff, listen to him. You can't go against Caldwell,' Emily pleaded.

He ignored her and looked at the mayor. 'Well? You need a sheriff. Do I get the job or not?'

Dean stared at me, and when I didn't move he looked at Jeff and nodded. 'The job's yours, Sheriff Harper.'

I heard Emily gasp with fear as I turned away.

'Trace, do something,' Meredith called to my back.

'Come on, Mer,' I called back over my shoulder. 'You can't cure stupid.'

'Who are you calling stupid, outlaw?' Jeff snapped harshly.

I stopped and turned. My eyes grew hard and I said in a low voice, 'If the shoe fits. By the way, you might want to get the undertaker to dig a fourth grave in the cemetery. You'll be needing it.'

Then I turned away once more and kept walking.

CHAPTER 7

Bren Deavers was in his study doing bookwork when word arrived about Brody and his deputies. He'd just opened a ledger to write the latest tally figures in, when a solidly built man wearing range clothes and a twin gun-rig entered the room.

Deavers looked up at him and could see the concern in his brown eyes.

'What is it, Rance?' Deavers asked.

Rance Caldwell was Deavers' foreman, troubleshooter, and hired gun. And the man responsible for the death of Joe Madden.

'One of the boys just came in from town,' he explained. 'Brody and his deputies are dead.'

Deavers froze. 'What happened?'

'It seems that Trace Madden is a little more capable than you expected,' Caldwell explained. 'They tried to gun him down in the main street of Blackmere and got killed for their trouble.'

Deaver's hand crashed down onto polished wood.

'I didn't want him dead. Just arrested and out of the way.'

'Well, it looks like he ain't going to be out of the way anytime soon,' Caldwell surmised.

'Damn it!' Deavers exploded. 'I want the son of a bitch out of the way before our guest arrives in a few days. I was hoping to have the ranch by then, too.'

Caldwell remained silent as he watched his boss walk across to a window and stare out across the rolling landscape, contemplating his next move.

He turned back and said, 'Find Madden and tell him I want to see him.'

Caldwell frowned. 'Are you sure?'

Nodding, Deavers said, 'Yes. Let's see how attached he is to that ranch.'

'All right, you're the boss,' he allowed. 'There is one other thing.'

'What?'

'She's with him.'

'Well that just changes everything, doesn't it?'

It was a somber affair, the ride back to the ranch, what with Emily crying over her soon to be dead beau and Meredith not talking to me. Sometimes you just can't tell people that they're in over their heads.

Once back, I went and took my frustrations out on a large pile of firewood. Bert found me shirtless and working up a good lather.

'Are you all right, son?' he asked me.

I buried the axe blade into the block and looked at him. 'What do you know about Deavers, Bert?'

He frowned. 'Only what I already told you. Why?'

'Caldwell doesn't just work for anyone,' I explained. 'He demands top dollar and most of the time he used to work for only one man. And his name wasn't Deavers.'

'Who was it then?'

Meredith suddenly appeared. 'His name is Gideon Blake. He is a cruel, mean, heartless son of a bitch. A man who should have been killed long ago.'

I looked at her. 'We don't know, Mer.'

'I do,' she stated flatly. 'Having someone dragged to death in barbed wire is something that bastard would do.'

I looked at Bert. 'Describe him.'

'Well, he's a solid built man, early forties, hair starting to go gray.'

Meredith's face said it all. 'I told you, didn't I?'

I nodded.

'Wait, you know this feller?' Bert asked, surprised. We both nodded.

'But how?'

Meredith said, 'He used to be my husband.'

'He used to be what?' Ma exclaimed. The shock of it made her sit down at the table.

'It's true, Ma,' I said. 'Gideon Blake and Meredith were married.'

'Oh, my Lord,' she sighed in bewilderment. Then she looked hard at me. 'Is all this something to do with you?'

I shook my head. 'I don't think so. Mind you, it is

62

mighty convenient though.'

'I didn't meet Trace until a year after I left Gideon,' Meredith explained. 'So I don't see how it could be.'

Bert came into the room with a troubled expression on his face. 'Rider coming in. Looks to be Caldwell.'

'Is he alone?' I asked him.

Bert nodded. 'Yeah.'

'I'd best go see what he wants then,' I suggested.

'Trace, be careful,' Meredith urged me.

I rubbed her shoulder. 'Get a rifle. If he starts something, you can shoot him.'

'Won't be no use doing that if you're dead,' she pointed out.

I smiled at her making light of the situation. 'At least I won't die alone then, will I?'

She stood on her toes and kissed me on the lips. 'You'd better not die on me.'

'I'll try my best,' I told her. Shifting my gaze to Ma, I said, 'Whatever happens, don't come outside. Mer will take care of you all.'

'You got a lot of faith in her, boy,' Ma said.

'It ain't the first time I've trusted her with my life, Ma,' I explained. 'Don't worry, everything will be OK.'

I walked outside and met Caldwell in the yard. He didn't bother dismounting, just sat saddle and said what he'd come to say.

'Been a while, Trace.'

I nodded. 'Not long enough, Rance. Is there

something I can do for you?'

'The boss wants to see you.'

'By boss, do you mean Deavers or Blake?'

He gave me a wry smile. 'I hear tell she's with you.'

'If you're talking about Meredith, then yeah, she's with me.'

'Never woulda took you for a wife stealer, Trace,' Caldwell said.

'I never stole her, you know that,' I corrected him. 'Never even laid eyes on her until a time after. Never even seen Blake until I was in Santa Fe one time, and that was from afar.'

'He knows all about you, Trace,' Caldwell allowed. 'I guess he still figures on getting his wife back sometime.'

'Is this what it's all about? The death of my brother? Was it a way of bringing me here so he could get Mer back?'

Caldwell shook his head. 'This ain't got nothing to do with you or her. And your brother had an accident. Nothing more.'

I thought for a moment. Then: 'All right, give me a moment. I'll come and hear what your boss has to say.'

I walked back inside and told them what I was about to do. Of course, it went down well, with Ma calling me all kinds of foolish and Meredith threatening to shoot me for being, in her words, 'a jackass'.

But there was no other way. I needed to know what I was up against, and talking to Deavers, or Blake, was the easiest way to find out.

'I see you came,' Deavers said from behind his desk. I guess he figured it some sort of position of power.

I nodded. 'What do I call you? Blake or Deavers?'

He gave me a cold smile. 'Let's stick to Deavers, shall we?'

'Sure, whatever.'

'How is my wife?'

It was my turn to smile. It hadn't taken long. 'She ain't your wife anymore.'

'She'll always be my wife,' he hissed at me.

'That's an unhealthy obsession you have there, Deavers,' I pointed out. 'Maybe you should just forget about it and move on. Meredith wants nothing to do with you.'

He leaned forward, placing his elbows on his desk. 'I'll move on when I'm ready. Not when you tell me to.'

It didn't take long for my patience to wane. 'Why am I here, Deavers? Tell me now or I'll leave.'

'That's what I want you to do,' he explained. 'I'm willing to forget about our past. . . .'

'We have no past,' I interrupted.

'. . . I'm willing to forget our past and leave Meredith alone, but in return, you both ride away from here.'

'Why do you want my family's land?'

'You don't need to know.'

'Well, hell, you obviously think it's all worth killing my brother for,' I pointed out icily.

'That was a tragic accident.'

I shook my head.

'All right then,' Deavers sighed. 'I'll give you ten thousand dollars to sweeten the pot.'

I was stunned. Obviously, there was a reason why he wanted the land, and he wanted it bad.

'It's a good offer, Trace. Why not take it?' Caldwell advised me. It was the first time he'd spoken since we'd entered the study.

I looked Deavers in the eye and said, 'I think I'll stay.'

His eyes flicked across to Caldwell who stood off to one side, the look warning me that I needed to act.

In a blur of movement that took both men by surprise, my Peacemaker came clear of leather and was level, cocked, and pointed at Caldwell's head before his gun had moved.

'Here I was thinking that this was a peaceable meeting between friends,' I said between gritted teeth. 'Tell me why I shouldn't kill you, Rance?'

'Because you ain't never shot a man down cold, Trace,' he answered, showing no outward emotion.

I turned my head and stared at Deavers. 'If you keep after my family, I'm apt to forget about my scruples. For now, I have more important things to do.'

'Like what?' Deavers snapped.

I fixed my gaze back on Caldwell. 'Like finding the son of a bitch who murdered my brother.'

'Good luck with that,' Caldwell offered.

I holstered my Colt. 'I don't need luck. I got me a

feeling he'll come to me when the time is right.'

That was where the meeting ended. I turned around and walked out. The only problem I had now was that there were more unanswered questions.

Later that evening, I was sitting on the buckboard tray with Meredith discussing the events of the meeting with Deavers.

'Why do you think he wants the land so bad?' she asked me.

'I don't know, but I intend on finding out. How's Emily doing?'

'She's really worried, Trace,' Meredith told me. 'She sure loves that young man. Can't you do something?'

'I'm going into town tomorrow to ask around about a couple of things. I'll check up on him while I'm there.'

'I'll come with you,' Meredith said hurriedly.

'I'd rather you stay here and keep an eye on things,' I told her.

'All right, but you stay out of the saloons. You know trouble always seems to find you in those places.'

'I promise I'll try to stay out of trouble.'

She eyed me warily. 'Make sure you do, Trace Madden. You promised we'd go to California. I aim to see that you keep it.'

Looking back, I should never have gone to town. That way I would have stayed out of the saloon and wouldn't have been involved in more gunplay. I wouldn't have been shot, and I wouldn't have had to face Meredith's wrath.

Hindsight is a wonderful thing.

Bren Deavers was still at his desk when Caldwell gave him the news about the new sheriff of Blackmere. His answer was to stare at Caldwell for a long period of time before saying, 'Send some men to take care of it tomorrow.'

'You want him dead?'

'Dead's easier.'

'OK then.'

CHAPTER 8

The following day I lay on the doctor's table, with a deep burning pain ripping through my body as he stitched the bloody tear in my hide. I cursed myself through gritted teeth for the fool that I'd been. I should have known there was a third gunman. My mind was telling me something was wrong and yet I'd missed it.

Now, here I was getting myself patched up and waiting for the sky to fall in.

When I'd arrived in Blackmere, the first place I'd called at was the lands office. After we got past the first few awkward moments, I found there what I expected to find. The lands agent told me, and showed me, that Deavers had every right to fence the water.

When I asked him if he knew why now, he replied, 'I asked him the same question. He told me he was doing it because he could.'

The telegrapher proved to be a little more difficult

69

to encourage talking. He was a pinch-faced little man with red hair and buckteeth.

When I walked inside his small office he greeted me without looking in my direction. 'I'll be with you in a minute.'

As I glanced around the room I saw something that made me smile: a Wanted poster with my name on it. Apparently I was worth $1,500. It was a shame that the artist hadn't taken time to find out what I actually looked like.

'What can I help you . . .' and he stopped there.

'That picture don't look nothing like me,' I said, indicating the poster.

The pale-skinned man blanched. 'Umm. What . . . what can I . . . umm . . .'

'I want to know if Deavers has sent any telegrams of late?' I asked, trying to alleviate some of his angst.

'You know I can't tell you that,' he said hesitantly.

'What can you tell me?'

'Nothing,' he insisted.

'Do you know of a reason why he's after my ma's land?'

He shook his head. 'Can't say.'

'So, you know something?'

Again. 'Can't say.'

'You must know something. There ain't much goes on around a town without the telegrapher knowing about it.'

His eyes flickered.

'I knew I was right,' I said evenly. 'What do you know?'

'Nothing.'

My hand dropped to the Peacemaker. 'Talk now, or by Christ, I'll plug you.'

I wasn't going to shoot him, but he didn't know that, and he held up his hands and blurted out, 'OK, I'll tell you what I know.'

'All right, speak.'

The words tumbled from his mouth. 'All I know is he has a feller coming in from Pennsylvania.'

'Who is he?'

'I'm not sure. I think his name is Heath.'

The name meant nothing to me. 'When?'

'I'm not sure. A few days maybe.'

'Where in Pennsylvania?'

He said, 'A place called Oil Creek Valley.'

Now that was interesting.

'Anything else?'

'No. It's all I know. Please . . .' he pleaded.

'All right. But if you hear anything else then let me know.'

He nodded vigorously. 'Yeah, sure.'

'And don't let on to Deavers that I was here asking questions,' I warned him. 'You don't want me to come back here mad.'

After that, I turned and left.

My next stop was the sheriff. After all, I did promise to check up on Emily's young man. I found him sitting in Pam's Eatery having his noon meal.

He looked up at me and appeared worried. Around a mouthful of food, he said, 'I'm not sure if I should run you out of Blackmere or arrest you.'

71

I pulled out a chair and sat on the opposite side of the table. 'Mind if I sit down while you decide?'

'Go ahead. I could be a while.'

I leaned forward. 'What do you know about Oil Creek Valley in Pennsylvania?'

'About where?'

'Oil Creek Valley in Pennsylvania,' I repeated.

Jeff gave me a dumb look. 'I ain't never heard of it.'

I sighed. 'OK, listen up, Sheriff. Oil Creek Valley in Pennsylvania is one of the biggest oil strikes in the country today. Now, what you need to ask yourself is why a man from there is coming in to meet with Deavers?'

Jeff put his fork down. 'A man from this Oil Valley place?'

'Yeah.'

'How do you know this?'

'A little bird on a telegraph wire told me,' I said.

'You forced the telegrapher to tell you, you mean,' Jeff guessed. 'I could lock you up for just that alone.'

My voice grew harsh. 'How about you take a breath? You got more to worry about than me. Deavers is up to something and you're on your own. Whatever it is, he's willing to kill to get it. My brother found that out. He offered me ten thousand dollars to ride away. That is how much he wants whatever it is. Now do you understand?'

'You think he's found oil out there somewhere?' he asked.

'Yeah, I do.'

72

Jeff remained silent, thoughtful under my gaze. Then he said, 'Maybe I need to go and have a chat with him.'

I shook my head. 'No. Don't let on we know about it just yet. I want to have a word to this Heath feller when he arrives.'

'Why should I listen to you?' Jeff asked abruptly. 'You're nothing but a common outlaw who should be arrested.'

I gave him an icy stare and growled, 'Kid, before this is over you may need me. Remember that. Just because you pinned on that star, it don't make you a man.'

Leaving him opened-mouthed, I turned and walked out. Hell, I needed a drink. Then I remembered Meredith telling me to stay clear of the saloons. I shrugged. What could go wrong?

What indeed?

When I sat at the table with the chipped top in the Palace, I couldn't help but notice some of the stares I was getting. I guess killing the local lawmen would draw that kind of attention.

The table I had chosen was sequestered away in a dim corner of the large room where most natural light didn't quite reach.

The barroom smelled of alcohol and tobacco smoke, of unwashed bodies and cheap perfume. And it was only one o'clock.

There was a card game in progress at a table near the front window and a few other customers lined up along the bar, two of which interested me with their behavior.

They were in deep conversation about something that they didn't want overheard, because every now and then one of them would look about to see if anyone was listening.

Then one of them, a tall, thin man, left.

I thought nothing more of it until he returned with the town sheriff in tow. That's when it all went south.

If he'd had more experience, I'd say that Jeff might have picked up that something wasn't right. Instead, he strolled right on into their trap.

Good thing I was there.

Good for him, bad for me.

'What the hell did you get me over here for?' I heard Jeff snap angrily.

'Mister Deavers decided that you're not the right man to wear the badge in this town anymore, Jeff,' one of them said. 'So we got you over here to ask you nicely to take it off.'

Like I said, if the young feller had any awareness about him, he'd have noticed the other man work his way around behind him. But he didn't and that just added to the issue he was about to face.

'I'm not taking this badge off and you can tell your boss to go to hell!' he exclaimed.

'How about you go there instead,' the man behind him snarled and commenced his draw.

My hand was resting on the Colt in my holster, and before the back-shooter had even finished what he was saying, I had it cocked and above the table.

From there I didn't hesitate. I squeezed the trigger and the hammer fell. The Peacemaker roared and my shot caught him in the side of his head, which snapped sideways, and he slammed against the bar, his gun falling to the floor as it spilled from his lifeless fingers.

I came to my feet and, as I did, my thumb ratcheted back the hammer once more. The sound from the previous shot seemed to still be bouncing off the walls when my Colt roared a second time.

This time the slug caught its intended target high up in the chest as he turned to face me. His gun wasn't level when the bullet from my own weapon drove deep and knocked him back. His finger reflexively depressed the trigger and the slug plowed into the floorboards, sending up splinters.

He collapsed in a heap at the foot of the bar and lay unmoving. I stepped around the table I'd been sitting at, smoking Colt still in my right fist.

I was concentrating on the men on the floor and didn't see the third man until it was too late. He'd been sitting off on his own. No sooner had I started forward when he came erect and the gun in his fist roared.

The impact of the slug as it ripped my side open spun me around and made me stagger. I struggled against the burning pain and brought my Colt up ready to fire once more.

Jeff, however, beat me to it and his own six-gun roared to life and the bushwhacker was flung back violently with an ounce of lead in his chest.

The noise as he crashed against chairs and a table, echoed throughout the saloon.

There were shouts of alarm from some of the drinkers and a saloon girl started to scream at the sudden violence and death. I looked across at her and snapped apathetically, 'Shut up. You ain't helping.'

I shifted my gaze to Jeff, who by now had a stunned expression on his face as well as the smoking six-gun in his hand.

'What the hell just happened?' he asked in a bewildered tone.

'What the hell do you think just happened?' I growled in anger. 'These bastards just tried to kill you because of that badge painting a target on your chest. If you've got any sense, you'll take it off.'

The pain in my side was getting worse and when I pressed my hand to it, it came away covered with blood.

I looked at him once more and through gritted teeth I hissed, 'You son of a bitch. You done got me killed.'

'What?' he blurted out and hurried across to where I stood. He looked at the bloody tear in my shirt and said, 'It don't look like it'll kill you.'

'It ain't the wound I'm worried about.' I mumbled and fell face first to the floor.

Which brings me back to the doctor stitching the ugly wound in my side and me cursing every dog-toothed one he made. It couldn't possibly get much worse, could it?

'Where in damnation are you, Trace Madden?' I heard the voice call out from the other room.

Yes, it could!

'You'd best give me some of that blasted chloroform you got, Doc,' I said hurriedly. 'Before she gets in here. Otherwise, my side ain't the only part of me you'll be stitching up.'

Too late. The door opened and standing there was Meredith, looking about as angry as I'd seen her in a good while.

Her eyes blazed and my first thought was, *damn, I love this woman*. It didn't last long though. My second thought was about the type of headstone I might need for my grave.

'What were my very last words before you left? Hmm?' she growled like a cougar circling its prey. 'Let me tell you. I told you to stay away from the saloons in Blackmere. But did you listen? Nooo. Sometimes I feel like I'm talking to myself.'

'It's a Madden male thing,' Ma said as she entered behind Meredith. 'Might as well talk to a post. His father and brother were exactly the same.'

If you've ever been trapped and outnumbered by a howling war party of Indians, then you'd have some idea of how I felt at that moment. And my best defense was, 'It weren't my fault.'

Meredith cast an angry gaze at Doc Grace and asked, 'Have you finished with him yet?'

'A couple more stitches and I'll be done,' he replied.

'Good,' she snapped and moved over beside him. She almost shouldered him out of the way and to my horror said, 'I'll finish them if you please. And before you ask, I've done this more than once.'

My gaze was pleading with him not to let her touch the needle and thread, but I saw something in the gray-headed, old man's eyes that gave me cause for concern. He was enjoying it.

I closed my eyes at the premonition of impending doom and my fears were realized when I heard him croak, 'Be my guest.'

CHAPTER 9

Two days later, I was recovering at the ranch when a rider appeared. I was outside at the corral when I noticed him. My side was stiff, and the stitches pulled a little, but I figured a few more days and I'd be fine.

It was Jeff Harper, duly appointed sheriff of Blackmere. He eased his horse to a halt and said, 'I see you're still alive.'

I nodded. 'I'm breathing. It was touch and go for a while though. Between Meredith and Ma, I thought I was in for a bloodletting.'

The door to the house went and I turned to see my sister and Meredith emerge. Emily hurried across to her beau and was upon him as soon as his boots hit the coarse, hard-packed earth of the ranch yard.

She drew back and said, 'Come inside. Ma has put some fresh coffee on.'

He smiled and said, 'I'll be there in a minute. But first I want to talk to your brother.'

Emily looked almost dejected, but she hurried

back inside anyway. Meredith, on the other hand, came across to where we were standing.

Jeff looked sideways at her, a nervous expression on his face.

'It's OK,' I said, trying to ease his angst. 'Meredith left her six-gun inside.'

He laughed nervously but when he saw Mer wasn't, he stopped quick smart.

'What did you want to see me about?' I asked him.

'I . . . ah . . .' he shot a sidelong glance at Meredith.

'Oh, for crying out loud,' she snapped, 'just get on with it.'

'OK, OK.' He blurted out, 'I want you to come on as my deputy.'

'No,' Meredith answered without giving me a chance to speak.

Now, as you know, I'm not all that fond of the law myself, but at that point in time, I could see that wearing a badge would have its advantages.

'I'll do it,' I told him.

Meredith's gaze grew hard as she looked at me, it saying, *didn't you hear what I just said?*

'Mer,' I said, 'he needs my help. They ain't going to rest while he's still wearing that badge. You know that.'

'Well tell him to take the damned thing off,' she snarled angrily. 'They almost killed you once already. I don't want them succeeding next time.'

'I'm doing it, Mer,' I said with finality. 'That's all there is to it.'

She growled at me from deep in her throat and stamped her foot before whirling around and stomping off.

'I didn't mean to get you into trouble,' Jeff apologized to me. 'It'll only be for a short while. I sent for a US Marshal.'

That was all I needed, federal law showing up. 'Don't worry about it. She'll be angry for a while, but she'll see that it's the right thing to do. Just give me a couple of days and I'll come into town.'

Jeff nodded. 'OK.'

Little did I know that at that point there was a storm coming, and at its center would be me.

Meredith was far from happy. Even later that afternoon while I was out at the corral feeding the horses, she tried again to talk me out of it.

'I don't like it, Trace. I want us to leave before it's too late.'

'It's already too late, Mer. Jeff needs my help.'

'Oh, you are so stubborn, Trace Madden,' she fumed.

I took her in my arms and stared into her tear-filled eyes. 'Caldwell and Deavers are behind the death of Joe. I know it. They're after the ranch and I have a feeling we'll find out why in the next few days. I can't leave now, you know that.'

Meredith placed her head against my shoulder. 'I just couldn't bear it if I lost you, Trace.'

'Outlaw and all?'

'Outlaw and all.'

81

It was almost as if I could feel the disturbance before I heard it. I looked up and saw two riders approaching the ranch house.

'Riders coming, Mer,' I said and eased her away from me.

She turned and stared in their direction. She squinted and said, 'Is that who I think it is?'

'Yeah, I think so. Blaze and Miller.'

'What on earth are they doing here?' Meredith pondered.

'More to the point, where's Frenchy?'

The duo rode into the yard, looking ragged and worn down.

'What happened?' I asked. There were no hellos. It was beyond that.

Blaze said, 'We screwed up, Trace. When you left we went and pulled a job on our own.'

I felt my blood begin to rise. 'Tell me about it.'

'It was my fault,' Blaze said. 'We thought – I thought that if we did it then you wouldn't need to do the other. You'd have enough money and that would keep Mer happy too.'

'What happened, Blaze?'

'Cleve Hardin had the same idea as we did. At the exact same time. Only we got away with the money after one of his men dropped it. They got arrested and we got away.'

'Where's Frenchy?'

Blaze went on. 'Somehow, Hardin and his men must've got away. They tracked us to the cabin. They killed Frenchy before we even knew they were there.'

82

I closed my eyes as my mind became filled with rampant thoughts. This wasn't good. Hardin wasn't a man to let things go and I knew that out there somewhere was an angry grizzly on a trail of blood.

I glanced at Meredith and saw a tear run down her cheek. I felt the same way. The gang had been together for a while now and we were all close friends.

'Do you know the worst of it, Blaze?' I asked. 'It's not the fact that you went and did this on your own. Nor that Frenchy died because you screwed up. The worst is that Hardin ain't going to stop until he finds you. And that means he's going to come *here* to my family's home.'

Realization dawned on Blaze. 'Oh, hell, I'm sorry, Trace. I didn't think.'

'Now that's twice. Don't let there be a third. Get your horses into the corral.'

I watched them go and felt Meredith move closer in beside me. I put my left arm around her and pulled her close.

'What are you going to do, Trace?'

'I don't know.'

At dinner that evening I'd made my decision and told Ma. 'We're leaving, Ma. Riding out tomorrow.'

My decision took everyone by surprise, especially Meredith and my mother. Perhaps I should have told her before I blurted it out.

'The hell you are, Trace,' she growled.

That's my ma; she sure has a way with words.

'My thoughts exactly,' Meredith chimed in.

'Adding Hardin to the mix has changed things. He won't stop until he gets what he wants.'

'What about doing what you said you would for Jeff?' Ma asked. 'You can't go back on your word now, Trace. We can look after ourselves. If that Hardin feller comes around here, he'll get what's coming to him. Besides, I've made a decision too. I'm going to drive some of the cows to market and sell them. For that I need you and your friends.'

'And Jeff needs you,' my sister pointed out.

'All right, we'll stay. But if you aim to make a drive, even a small one, you'll need water.'

'There's water in town,' Ma pointed out.

I chuckled. 'You can't take your herd into town.'

'There's a creek on the north side, dumbass. I'll take them there. We have to bypass town to move them to the railhead at Everton. I might as well fill them up there.'

That's Ma: resourceful. 'How many are you going to send?'

'Five-hundred should be enough. I'm hoping I can find enough water somewhere to get the rest through.'

I nodded. 'I'll get Blaze and Miller at it tomorrow. Maybe it'll keep them out of trouble.'

'You're not going to help them?'

'Nope. I have another job, remember?'

That evening, as we sat around the table, Cleve Hardin and his men rode into Blackmere on tired horses. However, their arrival didn't go unnoticed, but I sure as hell wished it had.

As they rode through the main street, Jeff happened to be out on patrol and caught a glimpse of them moving through the lantern light shining from a store window. He frowned and then looked worried as they passed. Something wasn't right.

He hurried back to the jail and found a thick bundle of wanted posters on the office desk. Thumbing through them, he'd gone through half the stack before finding the one he was looking for and held it up. That was him. Cleve Hardin.

He tossed it back on the desk, took a Winchester down from the gunrack, and stormed outside.

Finding their horses outside the saloon, he stopped at the doors and looked about. They were seated at a table in the corner. Jeff mumbled under his breath, 'Come on, do your job. It's what you're getting paid for.'

Looking back, I wish he had waited for me. But he didn't and things in town went from bad to worse.

Caldwell was at the bar when he saw Jeff Harper come into the room. He watched on in anticipation as he saw the young lawman turn left and approach the men at the table. 'You're green, kid, but you've got guts. And guts will get you killed,' he muttered.

Jeff stopped before the table and spoke in a loud voice, 'Cleve Hardin, you're under arrest.'

Hardin looked up and gave him a cold smile. 'Go away, kid, and take that pop-gun with you.'

'Can't do that. It's my job.'

'That's where you're wrong, kid,' Hardin sneered. 'It's your funeral.'

Beneath the table, the gun held by the outlaw roared and the polished timber on top of it exploded upwards. Slivers of wood showered Jeff and the misshapen bullet ripped into his chest. He staggered back, hit hard. Hardin came to his feet and fired again. This time the kid went down.

The killer stared at him and looked around the room. 'Anybody else try anything, they get what the kid got.'

Caldwell looked at Jeff and then at Hardin. He nodded. His boss could use these men for what was to come.

CHAPTER 10

When I rode into town the following morning, I could sense the foreboding that hung over it. All the citizens seemed to have slowed down, the total opposite of the normal bustling about their business.

I stopped at the jail and went inside. It was empty, so I went back out to the boardwalk. I thought Jeff must have been out doing rounds or something, but I soon found out otherwise.

'If you're looking for the sheriff, Trace, he ain't there,' said a thin man I remembered from when I used to live in town.

'Where can I find him, Mr Waylon?' I asked. No call not to be polite.

'He got himself shot last night over at The Red Queen. He's at Doc Grace's. It ain't good. Doc don't expect him to live.'

I was running before he got the last few words out. This was bad. Very bad.

When I arrived, I found the doc in his outer office.

'How is he, Doc?'

The worried expression on his face said it all. He gave a slight shake of his head. 'He's not good, Trace. I've done all I can.'

'What happened?'

'He braced some outlaws in the saloon last night. Four of them, can you believe?'

I could believe it. 'Who were they?'

'I don't know.'

I nodded. 'Where's his badge?'

The doctor turned away and opened a drawer in the cupboard behind him. When he turned back he had it in his hand. I took it and pinned it to my shirt.

'What are you doing?'

'He asked me to be his deputy. I agreed. But I guess I just got promoted. There should be a marshal coming in soon, I hope.'

'You be careful, Trace,' he cautioned me.

I stared at him, my anger roiling deep down in the pit of my stomach. I said in a low voice, 'We're beyond careful, Doc. Way beyond.'

As I walked along the street, I swear more than a few jaws dropped at the sight of the badge pinned to my chest. Who would have thought? An outlaw in their town wearing the sheriff's badge. When I reached The Red Queen, I strode in with purpose. The barkeep saw who I was and leaned down beneath the counter to grab what I assumed was a sawn-off shotgun.

My six-gun leaped into my hand and I put a slug

into the front of the bar. He sprang back and held up his hands.

'A mite jumpy, ain't you?' I pointed out.

'What else do you expect? You're a damned outlaw like those bastards last night.'

Obviously not one of my biggest fans. But I didn't care; I was here for answers. 'Who were they?'

'Hardin's bunch.'

My blood ran cold.

'Where did they go?'

He shrugged. 'I don't know. They talked to Caldwell for a short time and then he left. Not long after, they left too.'

It looked as though I was going to have to pay Deavers another visit. But first I had to go home and break the news to my sister. And that was something I dreaded.

I was right. Emily collapsed onto the ground and sobbed inconsolably. Ma crouched beside her, wrapping arms around my sister in her all-enveloping hug as she'd done to all of us at least once during our lifetime.

Meredith stared at me through tears of her own. 'Are you going after them?'

I nodded. 'If I can. Will you go with them to town?'

'Yes.'

'Have Blaze go with you.'

Meredith shook her head. 'No. He's too busy with the cattle.'

I nodded. She was right. 'OK.'

89

'Where are you going to start?'

'Deavers.'

Alarm flashed in Meredith's eyes. 'Oh, no, Trace. Not there.'

'If I want answers then I have to start there. Caldwell was seen talking to them.'

She knew I was right and nodded her agreement. 'You be careful, Trace.'

'You know me, Mer, I'm always careful.'

Deavers eyed the men before him. 'So, are you happy with my terms?'

Hardin nodded. 'Sure. You want us to sit around and when you call, we come running?'

'That's about it. You don't leave the line shack nor go to town or do anything without my say so. I'm sure I'll have work enough for you soon.'

'You're the boss.'

'I am. Just you remember it.'

Hardin bristled. 'That sounds like a threat to me, Deavers. But I must have been hearing you wrong.'

'It is what it is, Hardin.'

The outlaw glanced at Caldwell. He'd heard about the man's reputation, so he didn't want to push it. Yet.

'All right then, Mr Deavers. You holler and we'll come.'

'Good, now get out of here. Caldwell will show you where to go.'

Before I rode onto Deavers' range, I swung by to see

Blaze and Miller and tell them what had happened. Bert was there too, and my news didn't seem to surprise him in the least.

Blaze stared at me and shook his head. 'I'm sorry, Trace. This is my fault. I'll be gone by sundown if that's what you want?'

'Nope. What's done is done. The kid didn't have to brace them on his own.'

'Well then let us come with you.'

'You keep working the cattle. I'll be fine.'

I left them to it and rode across to see Deavers.

I'd no sooner crossed onto his land than some of his riders waylaid me. There were two of them. Tall, skinny string beans with mean frowns on their faces. They pointed a brace of Winchesters at me and said, 'What do you want, Madden?'

I stared at them and said, 'You fellers look like someone stole your best broncs. Not the sunny dispositions I was expecting.'

'Speak,' the one on the left said.

My horse shifted beneath me. 'I want to see your boss.'

They eyed me warily. The one who'd spoken before nodded. 'OK. But give us your gun first.'

I shook my head. 'Not going to happen.'

'Then you don't come no further.'

'I'll give you fellers a choice. Take me to Deavers or I'll shoot you where you sit.'

They both smirked at me. 'You wouldn't dare.'

I raised my eyebrows and said, 'Outlaw!'

They didn't know what to make of it and then

relented. 'OK. But any wrong moves and we'll bury you.'

It was my turn to smirk. 'You'll try.'

Meredith sat on an old stump near the ranch house and stared out across the landscape. She was so wrapped up in her thoughts that she didn't hear Ma come up beside her.

'You love my son, don't you?'

Meredith turned her head. 'Very much. He's everything to me.'

'So why are you both still living as outlaws?'

It was blunt, straight to the point. 'I've been trying to get him to quit for an age now. He kept telling me one last job and we'll have enough. Well, he was about to do that one last job when he found out about Joe. And here we are.'

'You know, he wasn't always a bad boy?'

'I don't think there's a bad bone in his body,' Meredith said. 'He may have done bad things but he's not bad.'

'What if I tell him to go?' Ma asked.

Meredith shook her head. 'You know what he's like. Do you think he'd leave with all this going on?'

'Nope.'

'Exactly. And that's what worries me.'

'What do you mean?'

'Jeff sent for a marshal,' Meredith explained. 'What do you think will happen when he arrives and finds Trace?'

Ma frowned. 'I see what you mean.'

Meredith's shoulders slumped, and the tears came. 'I'm afraid they'll kill him, Ma.'

Ma put her arms around Meredith and tried to soothe her anxiety. 'You shush child. I'll not lose another son of mine. Not now.'

When I arrived at the Broken D, there seemed to be a lot of hands in the yard. I drew up under the threat of guns and was about to climb down when a voice said, 'Stay where you are. You ain't been asked to climb down yet.'

Caldwell came out from under a low veranda and stood where I could see him. His hand rested on the butt of his six-gun. 'What do you want, Madden?'

'I want to talk to your boss.'

'Why?'

'Law business.'

It was then that he saw the badge on my shirt. He gave a derisive snort. 'Ain't that something. The outlaw has gone and turned lawman.'

The screen door opened and Deavers appeared. 'What do I owe the pleasure, Sheriff?'

'I want to know where I can find Hardin and his bunch,' I said.

'Don't know them.'

'Caldwell was seen talking to them right after young Jeff Harper was shot. Maybe he knows. Should we ask him?'

I shifted my gaze to the killer. 'Well?'

He shrugged. 'Sure. They said they were passing through. I told them it might be best seeing that the feller they shot was stepping out with the sister of the notorious outlaw Trace Madden.'

He smiled at me and I contemplated climbing down and wiping it from his face – probably not a good idea considering all the guns that were present.

'Where did they go, Caldwell?'

He shrugged his shoulders. 'Don't know.'

I stared at Deavers. 'If I find out you're behind the shooting, I'll come back and take you down.'

Deavers' anger flared. 'Are you threatening me on my own place?'

'Just telling you how it is.'

'Let me tell you how it is, outlaw. That badge don't change a thing. You're still the same Trace Madden.'

I eased my horse around and exposed my back to them. As I started to ride away I called back, 'Be seeing you, Bren.'

As I rode out of the yard I could feel their eyes boring into my back. At least it wasn't bullets.

CHAPTER 11

Two days later, the stage rattled into Blackmere while I was out turning over rocks to see if I could find Hardin and his gang. It was around mid-morning when the six-horse team trotted into town and drew up outside the livery stable where the driver was due to change teams.

An unseasonable morning storm had passed through the valley not long before, and mud was plastered up the sides of the coach as well as the horses' flanks.

The driver and the guard climbed down. One started to work on the team with the hostler while the other opened the doors to let the four passengers disembark.

There were two women and two men. One of the men hung around the back of the stage to collect his luggage. The shotgun guard, a man by the name of Withers, grabbed it for him and said, 'Here you go, Mr Heath. Hope you enjoyed your trip.'

Monroe Heath gave Withers a wan smile. 'Let's

just say that I'm not looking forward to the trip back. Could you recommend a good hotel?'

'There's one further along the main street. I think it's called Sunset Rooms or something like that.'

'Thank you.'

He leaned down and his jacket fell open. Withers noticed a gun in a shoulder holster. Maybe a double-action, .41 caliber Colt Lightning. Heath picked his bags up and started off along the street.

Checking into a room at the hotel, he was unpacked an hour later, before heading back to the livery to rent a horse. After getting directions to the Broken D, he rode out of town.

Just a quiet, inconspicuous man out for a ride. A man who was about to turn the valley upside down and bring the violence in the valley to a head.

'Rider coming in, Bren,' Caldwell called through the open door.

'Who is it?'

'No idea. Looks like a bit of a dandy, wears a suit. Could be that feller you're waiting on.'

'If it is, get me a horse saddled.'

'Sure.'

Heath eased his horse down and let it walk into the yard. When he stopped he looked at Caldwell and asked, 'Is this the Broken D?'

The gunhand nodded. 'Sure is. You Heath? The oil feller?'

'I am.'

'Go inside, the boss is expecting you.'

Heath found Deavers in the study, who came to his feet from behind his handcrafted desk and said, 'Mr Heath, I'm Bren Deavers. Pleased to meet you.'

They shook and Deavers offered him a drink.

'No, thank you, Mr Deavers. Not while I'm conducting business.'

Deavers nodded. 'OK, then. Shall we go and take a look at what you came to see?'

'Yes. I think so.'

'Well?' Deavers asked.

Heath looked down at the small black pool. He raised his head and looked about the surrounding landscape and then asked, 'You said there are another six like this?'

'There are.'

'I wish to see them.'

Deavers hesitated. Then he said, 'I can show you another three.'

'Why not the others?'

'They're not exactly on my land.'

'Well, show me what you can then.'

Over the next hour, Deavers and Caldwell showed the oil man the other deposits. After he'd seen the last, he asked, 'Where are the other three?'

'Do you see the gully about half a mile distant near that hill?'

'I do.'

'There's one there and another perhaps five-hundred yards beyond it.'

'Very interesting.'

'What is?'

'Well, Mr Deavers, from what I can tell, there is a sizable oil deposit beneath the ground here. So much so that I would go as far to say that it seems likely to be bigger than the one in Pennsylvania. Which, I might add, at the moment is producing over sixteen-thousand barrels per day. Mind you, we wouldn't be able to tell until we started to drill.'

Deavers couldn't keep the expression of excitement from his face. 'That's wonderful news, Mr Heath.'

'However, I imagine that to take full advantage of the field, my employer would like whatever is on the other side as well. Maybe I should enter into negotiations with whoever owns the land there.'

Alarm ran through Deavers. 'That won't be necessary, Mr Heath. I'm currently negotiating with the owner to acquire it.'

'How soon can we expect to find out?'

'Within the week, I should imagine. They are taking a little more persuading than I anticipated.'

Heath nodded. 'I understand. Do you need any more men to help the situation along?'

Deavers was shocked at first. 'What are you saying?'

'I'm asking whether you understand what I've just told you. There are millions of dollars out there just waiting to be taken from the ground. My employer and I are willing to provide any assistance required to achieve the desired result.'

'I think we can manage it, Mr Heath. But if we have any problems I'll be sure to let you know.'

I looked over the herd that had been gathered so far and said to Blaze, 'Looks good.'

'Yeah. We should be ready to move them to town tomorrow, water them, and then push them north. It would be better if we got no more rain. I hate getting wet.'

'Yeah. You want me to come along?'

He shook his head. 'No. We'll take care of it. There'll only be around five-hundred head like Ma wanted. We can hire an extra hand.'

'All right, I—'

What started out as a distant rumble grew louder until the ground beneath my horse started to shake. The animal began to get skittish and dance around. The cattle milled restlessly and nearby trees swayed with the movement. Then the tremor subsided.

'That was weird,' Blaze said. 'What was it?'

'Earth tremor,' I told him. 'We used to get lots of them around here when I was a kid.'

'You can keep them.'

'What do you reckon he's doing?' Blaze asked.

I was confused. 'Who?'

'Him up there on the hill,' Blaze said, pointing at the figure on a horse atop a rise to the west.

I reached down and drew the Winchester from the saddle scabbard. I jacked a round into the breech and said, 'How about I go and find out.'

I kicked my horse into a canter and pointed it towards the hill. I'd travelled no more than halfway when the rider turned his horse and headed down the other side of the slope.

When I crested the rise, there was no sign of the rider at all. Just a maze of gullies and trees, any one of which he could have taken. All led back to the Broken D.

I thought about following him but then dismissed the thought. It could be a trap to get me into the gullies where whoever it was waited to ambush and shoot me.

I sat there for maybe ten minutes but saw nothing. Then I gave my shoulders a shrug and turned my horse back towards the herd.

'You find out who it was?' Blaze asked me when I got back.

I shook my head. 'If I had to guess, I'd say it was one of Deavers' men.'

'Probably keeping an eye on what we're doing.'

I nodded. 'Just keep your eye on them. I'm headed to town to check on Jeff. I'll see you tonight.'

When I arrived to see the doctor, I found Emily there as she'd been for the past few days: seated beside his bed.

'How's he doing?' I asked her.

She climbed from the chair and wrapped her arms around me. 'Oh, Trace. There's no change.'

I let her go and stared into her teary eyes. 'He's tough, Em. He's got this far.'

She nodded and took up her vigil beside the bed again.

I slipped out to see Doc Grace. 'How's he doing, Doc?'

The man shrugged. 'He isn't dead, which in itself is a good sign. I wish I could tell you more, but I can't.'

I nodded. 'He just seems to be hanging in there.'

'Yes, and the longer he does that, the better the prognosis might be.'

The door opened and I turned to see Meredith entering with a basket in her hands. She gave me a smile. I hadn't seen her since leaving earlier that morning. She gave me a kiss on the cheek and her sweet smell lingered after she pulled away.

'Will you be home for dinner?' she asked. 'I think your ma is cooking a feast to try and help us forget what is going on, even if it's just for a short time.'

'Are you going to be there?' I asked.

'Of course.'

'Then I wouldn't miss it for the world.'

'How's Jeff doing?'

I shrugged. 'Hanging in there. Is that for me?'

Meredith tapped me on the arm. 'Not likely. Your ma sent it in for Emily.'

I nodded towards the door. 'Through there. You want to meet me for a late lunch when you're done?'

She smiled. 'Sure.'

'I have something to check on, but say I meet you at Katie's in an hour?'

She kissed me on the cheek again and said, 'I'll be there.'

*

I headed over to the livery where the stage came in of a day. The morning one had been and gone and I found the hostler doing out stalls. 'Anyone get off the stage this morning?'

He spit on the floor and I wondered if it was directed at me. 'Yeah. Dandy looking feller.'

He turned away and kept at his work.

'You get a name?'

'Nope.'

'You know where he went?'

'Hotel.'

'Which one?'

'Sunset Rooms.'

I turned to leave when he said. 'He ain't there, though.'

'What do you mean?'

'He rented a horse and headed out to the Broken D.'

'How long ago?'

'Not long after the stage got in.'

'Thanks.'

From there I went over to the hotel. I found a young desk clerk behind the counter who watched me enter, his wary eyes never leaving me.

When I reached the counter he took a step back. I stared at him and said, 'A feller got off the stage today and came here for a room.'

'Ah, yes, sir.'

'What was his name?'

'I'm not sure.'

I pointed at the register. 'Can I have a look at that?'

He hesitated. 'Not really—'

I reached out and took it anyway.

'. . . yes, I guess that's fine.'

I ran my finger down the page until I found the name Heath. So the oil company man had arrived. I looked up. 'Thanks.'

'Sure, any time.'

Something that I doubted very much.

I knew the sun couldn't go down on the day without some kind of trouble. Sure, there was the rider watching the round up earlier, but that was nothing, really. However, Meredith and I had just finished our late lunch when two men entered the small eatery.

They were loud and running off at the mouth, and what other table would they choose to sit at but the one next to ours? What really irked me was the way they both openly leered at Meredith.

'Howdy, ma'am,' one of them said. 'Enjoy your meal?'

I knew she could take care of herself, but over the past couple of days I'd seen a change in her that I couldn't put my finger on. Instead of being the sharp-tongued, quick-witted woman I knew her to be, she'd become more reserved. I found out later that it was all because of me. Ma would explain later about the fears Mer had that this episode with Deavers could be my final hurrah. But right at this point, I had no idea.

'Yes, thank you,' she said.

'You could join us, ma'am, if you wish,' the other

one said.

'No, thank you.'

I frowned at her and she gave me a warning glance along with a slight shake of her head.

That wasn't like her at all.

'Hey, ma'am—'

'Enough,' I said in a quiet voice, full of menace.

Meredith's eyes widened and she reached across the table to grasp my hand.

'You got something to say, mister?' the one who'd spoken first asked.

'Trace,' Meredith said quietly. 'Let it go.'

'What's wrong, Mer?'

'Just leave it.'

'Cat got your tongue, cowboy?'

I grasped Meredith's hand with my free one and let it linger atop hers. She gave me a gentle smile.

'Not much of a man you got there, missy. Maybe you should join us at that.'

Meredith rolled her eyes for she knew what was about to happen. I removed her hand from mine and came to my feet.

'Trace, don't.'

'I promise I won't hurt them much, Mer.'

'It's not them I'm worried about.'

Too late, they realized they were in trouble. By the time they started to scramble for their guns, I'd already drawn mine.

With a backhanded sweep, the Colt hammered into the mouth of the man on the right. Teeth broke and blood flowed. The other smartmouth had his head slammed forward onto the table when I grabbed a handful of his hair with my left hand.

His nose broke in a spray of blood and he gasped as pain ripped through his face. Both of them slumped to the floor, a pair of bleeding messes.

I turned back to face Meredith and saw the expression on her face. It was one I'd often seen on Ma's face when I was growing up.

'What?'

'They never meant any harm, Trace. There was no need for that.'

'They'll mean even less then next time, won't they?'

Her eyes flared. 'Damn you, Trace Madden,' she said and stomped out.

CHAPTER 12

'Vickers is here to see you, boss,' Caldwell interrupted Deavers, who was doing paperwork. 'Says there's something going on over at the Madden spread.'

Deavers looked up. 'OK, show him in.'

A few moments later, Vickers entered the study. He sniffed the air and could smell the cigar smoke which lingered from earlier. He smiled at his employer. 'A man could sure get used to that smell. Yes, sir.'

Deavers rolled his eyes and reached across his desk to a small wooden box. He flipped the lid and took out a cigar.

'Here,' he said and tossed the cigar to Vickers.

The man's eyes lit up. 'Thank you, Mr Deavers.'

He ran it under his hawkish nose and breathed in its aroma.

'All right, tell me what you have to say and get out.'

'Sure. The Maddens are herding some of their

cows together. If I had to guess I'd say they're getting ready to make a drive.'

'How soon do you figure before they are ready?' Deavers asked.

'I guess they might be leaving tomorrow.'

'All right, thanks. Goodbye.'

Short and sweet. Deavers had no time for those who worked for him except for Caldwell.

After the door closed, the hired gun asked, 'What do you think?'

'I guess they're cutting down their stock until after the drought,' Deavers proposed.

'There was rain this morning.'

'Not enough to put water where it's needed. But I think we can take advantage of the situation.'

Caldwell nodded. 'You want us to hit the herd?'

'Yes, but only after it is has travelled a day or so beyond Blackmere. Actually, have Hardin do it and then hide them in the gullies and such in the foothills. From there we can ship them to market when it dies down.'

'I'll ride over first thing in the morning and tell him.'

Deavers continued. 'After they hit the herd, Madden will go looking for them. That'll give us the opportunity to hit the ranch house. I'm sick of waiting. I want it burned to the ground.'

'I'll see to it.'

'No, have Hardin do that too. He may as well earn his pay. At least that way it can't be physically linked back to us.'

'OK. I'll see to it. But you know once this happens, Madden is likely to come gunning for someone.'

Deavers shrugged. 'If he does, then you can have him.'

'And you'll have the woman.'

'Well, she was my wife once, why not again?'

For a meal that was supposed to cheer up the family, it was a pretty somber affair. For me anyway, since Meredith still wasn't talking.

I was helping Ma with the dishes and she asked, 'What did you do this time?'

With a look of feigned innocence, I said, 'What makes you think that?'

Sarcasm dripped from her voice, 'Yes, Trace Madden, I wonder what?'

I sighed. 'There was an incident in town today.'

She gave me an exasperated sigh. 'There's always an incident with you.'

I tried changing the subject. 'Tell me, Ma, what is going on with Mer? Has she said anything to you?'

'I swear, boy, you're blind to some things just like your pa was. Joe was the same.'

'How about you spare me the talk and tell me what it is.'

'You're a blind fool, Trace Madden—'

'Ma!'

'All right. She's afraid.'

'What?'

'I said she's afraid.'

'Of what?'

THE OTHER MADDEN

Ma shook her head. 'Not of what, for who? And that who is you. She's afraid you'll go and get yourself killed before this is done, when all she wants to do is go somewhere and settle down with you. Maybe even have a family.'

I brushed the worry off. 'Hell, I ain't going to go and get killed.'

Ma's eyes flared. 'How do you know that? Huh? How? I don't know that. Mer definitely doesn't. Hell, do you think Joe knew he was going to die the day he did?'

I was starting to get riled. 'What would you have me do?'

'Leave. Take Mer with you and damned well leave.'

'I can't do that.'

'Too damned stubborn is your problem.'

'I wonder where I got that from,' I almost shouted, and stormed off.

I was outside on the veranda, looking at the last vestiges of an orange sunset fade, when Meredith came out. I ignored her because I wasn't ready for another confrontation. She said, 'Are you OK? I heard you and your mother.'

'I'm fine,' I said, sounding suspiciously like a sulky child.

Meredith moved in beside me and looped her arm through mine. 'She's right. I'm scared, Trace. Scared you'll be killed and I'll be left alone.'

I opened my mouth to speak but she cut me off. 'Don't tell me you'll be fine. You don't know that.'

I shrugged. 'I can't stop now, Mer. It's gone too far.'

Meredith rested her head on my shoulder and said, 'I know. But promise me you'll be careful.'

My arms went around her waist. I turned her gently and raised her face to mine, staring into those eyes as I'd done so many times before and lied. I knew there are some promises you just can't keep. 'I promise.'

'Do you think you should say sorry to your mother?'

I winced. 'She'll be fine.'

Meredith elbowed me in the ribs.

'Hey, what was that for?'

She stepped back and glared at me.

I held up both of my hands. 'All right. All right.'

The thudding of hoofs sounded and I turned to look across the yard towards the gate. A man and horse came thundering through and he hauled back on the reins. The horse skidded to a halt and the rider came out of the saddle in swift movements.

I could see that he was anxious about something and when he spoke it was fast, panicked.

'Sheriff, you gotta come back to town. They robbed the bank around closing time.'

'Damn it!' I cursed. 'Who was it?'

'The Hardin gang. He said to make sure you knew who did it.'

'I'll be right with you.'

'They killed a teller, Sheriff. Just shot him down.'

'Head back to town and put word out that I want volunteers for a posse. Have them meet me at The Palace.'

110

With a bound he was back in the saddle and away towards town at a dead run. I turned to Meredith. 'I gotta go.'

'I know.'

Blaze came outside. 'What's the noise all about?'

'Hardin robbed the bank. I'm riding back to town.'

'I'll come with you.'

'No. Get that herd going in the morning, stop to water them in town, and then push on. OK?'

'Sure, Trace.'

'Saddle my horse for me?'

'Yeah, I'll do it now.'

He ran over to the corral and I turned to Meredith. I wrapped my arms around her then kissed her on the lips. 'I'll be back.'

'Make sure you are, Trace Madden.'

CHAPTER 13

Arriving in town, I went straight to the saloon. When I walked inside, it was all but bare. Instantly I felt my anger build within me. The man who'd come to the ranch was standing near the bar talking to the barkeep.

'Where's the posse?' I asked him.

He gave me a sheepish look. 'No one would volunteer.'

'What?' I was shocked. 'These outlaws rode into town and robbed the bank, and no one wanted to get their money back?'

Then I remembered I was one such person. Except for the killing part. My gaze fixed on him. 'Are you coming with me?'

'You're still going? In the dark?'

'I am.'

He hesitated.

'What's your name?'

'Elsom Monk.'

'I could use your help.'

Again he hesitated. I turned and walked towards the door.

'Wait, Sheriff,' he called after me. 'I'll ride with you.'

I nodded. 'OK. And call me Trace or Madden.'

'Yes, sir.'

So we rode out to find Hardin and his gang. Come morning, however, we were still empty-handed and knew not where they had gone.

'Of all the stupid things to do!' Caldwell seethed as he stared at the mound of money on the table. 'You were told to stay here.'

'You didn't just call me stupid, did you?' Hardin said in a soft voice. He dropped his hand to his gun butt.

'Get your hand off your gun, Hardin,' the gunman snarled. 'You don't scare me.'

'Tell me what you want and then get gone, Caldwell,' Hardin snapped.

'Deavers wants you to steal a herd of cattle.'

'When?'

'Late today, early tomorrow. It'll be north of town.'

'What are we supposed to do with them?'

Caldwell explained to them about where Deavers wanted them hidden.

'What then?'

'Once you've hidden the cows, you're to double back to the Madden place and hit their spread the next night. Burn it to the ground. I'll come with you.'

'What about those that are there?'

'What about them?'

'Nothing, I guess.'

'There is a woman there. Nothing should happen to her.'

'How will we know her?'

Caldwell described Meredith to them.

'What is she to Deavers?'

'You'll find out if anything happens to her.'

It was late morning when we rode back into town on tired horses. I'd known it was a long shot going out at night, but even in the morning light there was no sign. Especially after the shower of rain that had come through in the darkest hours. Maybe the drought was about to break after all.

Blaze and Miller, along with Bert, had the cattle at the creek having a drink before they pushed on north.

'They don't look to be in bad shape,' I observed.

Bert came over to me. 'They're tough stock. How'd you go tracking them outlaws?'

I shook my head. 'Even less chance of finding them now after the rain last night.'

'Tell me something,' Bert asked. 'I have been curious. What are you going to do when this marshal feller turns up?'

I cursed under my breath. I kept forgetting about that. It was a good question. 'I don't know, Bert.'

'Something to think about, son.'

'Right at this moment, I've got other things on my mind.'

114

He smiled at me.

'What are you smiling about?'

'You, an outlaw, thinking about the law. Working for it, in fact.'

'Yeah, well, I ain't going to make a habit of it. Be careful on the trail. You never know what's around the bend.'

'You watch your back too, son.'

'I always do.'

They say bad things come in threes, but for me it came in fours, fives, and sixes. Which is why I shouldn't have been surprised by what happened next, but I was when it did.

When I entered the jail, I found a man waiting for me. He was tall, solidly built, with a weathered face that spoke of a life outdoors. What's more, he was seated behind the office desk.

Then I saw the badge and my blood ran cold.

He looked me up and down and said, 'They told me you were out chasing outlaws. I didn't know how long you'd be so I made myself at home.'

I didn't say anything, just nodded.

'Did you have any luck?'

'Nope, Hardin and his bunch got away.'

'Bad feller that Hardin.'

'One of the worst.'

'My name is Bannon, by the way. Greg Bannon.'

'Uh-huh.'

'Didn't catch yours.'

'Nope. But I figure you already know it.'

He nodded and confirmed my suspicions. 'Before you think about going for your gun, you need to know mine is already out under the desk and pointed towards you.'

'I figured as much.'

He raised it above the desk and trained it on my middle. I could see that the hammer was cocked.

'Where do we go from here?' I asked him.

'About ten feet that way,' he said, motioning towards the cell.

I shrugged. 'Oh well, it was only temporary. I suppose you don't know how the kid is?'

'He woke up early this morning. I already talked to him. That's how I know who you are.'

'Then I guess you know why I'm doing it, too?'

'Yeah. Don't make much difference though.'

'Didn't expect it would.'

He locked me up after that. Then, while I had my feet up in Hotel Iron Bar, things went from bad to worse. And I could do nothing about it.

CHAPTER 14

Late that afternoon, just before the sun disappeared beyond the western mountains, the first of the calamitous events occurred.

Blaze had the herd bedded down five miles north of town, by a small stream fed from a spring way up amongst the jagged peaks to the west.

Miller was riding the herd with a young cowboy Blaze had hired. I'd find out later that his name was Brewer.

Miller was on the far side of the herd when the first shots sounded. One moment the night was relatively quiet, the next, three shots rang out followed by a cacophony of them.

Soon, the herd lunged to their feet and were running hard for the camp. Blaze came out of his bedroll and shouted at Bert.

'Stampede! Get up!'

Being older, Bert was a little slower. And it was that tardiness that left him in the path of over two thousand slashing, gouging, stomping hoofs.

With a brief cry of alarm, the first beast hit Bert flush in the back. He went down, and the rest of the herd trampled him into the ground.

Blaze managed to reach his horse and get mounted before the first beeves reached him. One cannoned into the mount and pushed it sideways. Blaze was almost unseated but managed to grab a handful of mane and stay upright.

The rest of the herd swept around his horse as the beast threw its head around, eyes rolling.

Then they were gone.

On the far side of the herd, Miller and Brewer rode towards the front of the bawling mass to try and get it stopped. In the moonlight, Miller saw some riders coming towards him. He couldn't make them out, but he knew it wasn't good.

Then the orange muzzle flashes started, and he could make out the faint pops of the gunshots over the thunder of hoofs.

Miller was hit hard and flung back over his horse's rump. He hit the ground and the air was expelled from his lungs. He tried to gather himself and fought to get to his feet. Suddenly a rider appeared before him, and a cold shiver ran through his body as he registered what was about to happen.

The gun in the rider's fist barked and Miller was shot for the second time. This time though, there was no getting up.

Brewer shouted when he saw the cold-blooded murder of Miller and drew his six-gun. He rode hard towards the killer. He fired a couple of shots and then his horse cannoned into the outlaw's mount. Both horses went down, spilling their riders from the saddles.

The outlaw recovered first and as Brewer struggled to his feet he was shot in the chest. Brewer went up on his toes and then all the strength left his body as he collapsed on the churned-up earth.

Blaze was the only man left and he was fighting a spooked horse, bareback. He'd only just got the thing under control after the rumble of hoofbeats disappeared into the distance. He cursed under his breath and then realized he wasn't alone. He hipped about in the saddle and saw the figure sitting his horse only a short distance away.

The gun flamed in the killer's hand and Blaze felt the slug slam into him. He fell from his prancing horse and lay there on the ground. Through eyes blurred by pain, he looked up at the figure still sitting there on his horse. Then the world seemed to spin, and he passed out.

It was Ma who brought me the news the following morning. Meredith had wanted to do it herself, but Ma talked her out of it. Although we'd tried to keep her identity a secret with every job she was involved in, you never could tell.

She told me of the deaths of Bert, Miller and Brewer, and how Blaze had brought her the news, wounded but still alive. He'd managed to catch a horse and somehow get astride it. When he arrived at the ranch, he was more dead than alive but still managed to tell them what had happened.

I stared across at Bannon through the bars. 'Hey, Bannon, you hear that?'

'I heard.'

'What are you going to do?'

Bannon came to his feet from the chair behind the desk. 'I guess I could go out and have a look. But that would mean leaving you here alone. When I come back, you might not even be here. Can't have that, can I? Therein lies my dilemma.'

'Then let me out of here and I'll go after Hardin myself.'

He shook his head. 'You don't even know if it was him.'

'I'm damned well certain of it. They shot the sheriff, robbed the bank, and now they've stolen the herd. Our herd. I'm also certain that the son of a bitch is working for Bren Deavers. With the money from the herd, it would have tied the ranch over until the next decent rain. But Deavers wants the ranch for himself. Killed my brother for it too, he did.'

'Seems to me that name was mentioned when I was assigned this job. Why does he want your land?'

'Oil.'

Ma looked at me like I was crazy. 'Oil?'

'Yeah. He had a feller come out here from Pennsylvania. Came in on the stage and went out to the Broken D. My guess is that it's on his land as well as ours. That's why he wants it so bad.'

'Who is this feller?' Bannon asked.

THE OTHER MADDEN

'His name is Heath.'

He gave me a skeptical look.

'Check it out. Go over to the hotel and look for yourself.'

Bannon nodded. 'All right, I'll check it out.'

'What about Hardin?'

'That'll have to wait.'

My frustrations went through the roof but a warning glance from Ma helped me hold them in check. Bannon disappeared, and I stared at Ma. 'How's Mer doing?'

'She's worried,' Ma said. 'That set in right after her anger let up. Man, I swear that girl must have some of my blood in her from times past. She's a hellfire when she gets wound up. She took up your pa's shotgun and was set on coming into town to bust you out. If I hadn't talked her out of it, she would've done just that.'

I smiled. 'She's a firebrand, all right.'

'You'd best marry her when this is all over.'

I smiled again. 'If I ain't breaking rocks in the pen, I will.'

Ma's face fell. 'Oh, yes. I forgot.'

My face grew serious. 'I'm sorry about Dert, Ma.'

She gave a somber nod. 'Me too. He was a good hand and friend. I could always depend on him.'

'Have you ever thought about what happens when all this is over, Ma?'

'How do you mean?'

'Why don't you come to California with Mer and me, all of you? Emily, Ruby and the boy.'

There was that *you're crazy* look again. 'And leave all that we'll have fought for? What your brother died for?'

'Sell it and buy another place out west, Ma. I'm not saying sell it to Deavers. That son of a bitch will be long gone by then. I could work it for you, and maybe Blaze will too. Mer and I would get married and you could enjoy time with Ruby and the boy.'

'I don't know, Trace.'

'Would you think about it? Ask Ruby and Emily?'

'What about Jeff? Your sister is hung up on that boy something fierce.'

'Hell, bring him too.'

She stared at me for a long time before she said, 'I'll think about it, Trace.'

I smiled. 'Good.'

'Don't go getting all excited just yet. I ain't said yes. And you're still in here.'

The door opened and Bannon stared at the man before him. 'Are you Heath?'

The man stared at the badge and nodded. 'I am.'

'Good. Mind if you tell me what you're doing in town?'

'I'm on business.'

'Oil company business?'

'Why would you say that?'

'You do work for an oil company, don't you?'

Heath nodded. 'I do.'

'Then I ask you again: why are you here in Blackmere?'

'I'm on business.'

'With Bren Deavers?'

'Never heard of him,' Heath lied.

Bannon sighed. 'Let me give you a bit of friendly advice, Mr Heath. There's a storm on the horizon that you'd find best to stay out of. I'd suggest that you climb aboard the next stage out of town and go back to where you come from.'

Heath smiled. 'Sounds like some fine advice, Marshal. But my company doesn't pay me to ride away from trouble.'

Right then and there, Bannon realized that there was more to this man than met the eye.

Bannon nodded. 'All right. Don't say you weren't warned.'

When Bannon returned to the jail, Ma and I were exactly where he'd left us. He seemed almost surprised that we were.

'I had me a talk to that feller over at the hotel,' Bannon said. 'Shifty he is.'

'So, you believe me?' I asked.

'Maybe. But I ain't letting you out of here. You're wanted in more places than water in a desert.'

'What are you going to do about the herd and the murder of the men with it?' I asked.

He just stared at me. I shook my head. Christ, I'd have to do it myself, but I was kind of detained.

CHAPTER 15

That night, with me waylaid in jail, Blaze wounded and the womenfolk on their own, Bren Deavers ordered his killers to burn Ma's ranch house.

Everyone had been asleep when the riders came out of the darkness. Hardin and his men were still on a high after taking the herd, so when the order came through to burn the ranch, there was no stopping them. I would find out later that they were led by Caldwell. The others who rode with them were hired hands. Deavers had changed his plans after I'd been locked up and the stealing of the herd had been so successful.

Meredith had heard them. She'd been awakened by the far-off rumble of hoofbeats, which grew steadily louder and brought her from the bed.

She walked across to the window and peered out through the curtain. At first, she saw nothing, then a faint orange pinprick that seemed to bob in the air. As the riders grew closer the orange pinprick separated into two, then four.

A rush of adrenaline coursed through her body. 'Nightriders.'

Meredith ran through the house calling out, waking Ma and Emily from their sleep.

They appeared not long after Meredith had grabbed a Winchester '76 from the gun rack. All of them were dressed in their nightclothes.

'What is it?' Ma asked.

'Nightriders. They've got torches. They're going to burn the house.'

Emily looked horrified. 'What about Blaze? If they set the house on fire—'

'The hell they're going to burn my house,' Ma said as she took down a rifle for herself. She grabbed another and gave it to Emily, then found three boxes of ammunition, which she distributed. 'I'll see them in Hades before they do that.'

There was movement at the doorway that led through to the room where Blaze was laid up. He appeared in the opening and leaned against the jamb. 'What's going on?'

Meredith told him and he nodded. 'Get me a gun.'

'You're too weak,' Meredith told him. 'Get back into bed.'

He shook his head. 'I'm strong enough to fire a damned gun.'

'Get him one,' Meredith snapped.

She loaded the Winchester and levered a round into the breech of the weapon. Outside, she heard the horses thunder into the yard. She looked at Ma and said, 'Cover me from the window.'

Then she went outside.

Each rider wore a flour sack over their head. They sat there on their horses, four of them with flaming torches. Meredith stood before them with the Winchester in her hands, cocked and ready to blow out the guts of the first man who moved.

'Seems to me you fellers are hard of hearing,' she growled in her fiercest voice. 'I said for you to turn your horses around and get out of here.'

'Move, girlie, or I'll shoot you where you stand,' one of the masked men snarled.

Meredith shifted her gaze. All of them were illuminated by the torches. Her stare settled on the speaker. 'Is that you, Cleve Hardin? Something I'd expect of a yeller backshooter like you.'

One thing about Meredith, she wasn't one to mince words.

'She won't shoot,' one of the other riders said.

'I shot Trace once,' she warned them.

They hesitated for a moment, uncertain whether she was telling the truth.

'Burn it,' Hardin snapped.

One of the men moved his horse forward to throw his torch up on the roof. It was the last thing he ever did.

The Winchester barked and the slug from it hit the hooded rider in the chest with enough force to blow him back over his horse's rump. Meredith worked the lever and brought the weapon up to fire at another of the riders. By now, panic tore through their ranks. They'd not expected her to shoot. They were sorely mistaken.

The second bullet slammed into another torch holder and ripped through the man's neck. His scream turned into a wet gargle as his thoat filled with blood. The six-gun in his hand dropped to the ground.

That was when the rest in the house opened fire. Ma killed one of Hardin's men herself and Emily brought down one of Deavers' hands. Blaze shot a second one, and then the chaos stepped up a notch as the would-be arsonists got their weapons working.

Meredith ran for the door as bullets hammered into the front of the house all around her. She rushed in breathlessly and slammed it shut, slugs beating a staccato drum on it as they tried to chase her through.

Ma said, 'Damn it, girl, who taught you to shoot like that?'

'I've had practice shooting at your son,' Meredith answered her.

'It's true,' Blaze called out as he fired another shot. 'Get Trace to show you the scar on his rump.'

It must've occurred to him what he'd just said and he followed it with, 'Or maybe not.'

Ma smiled. I guess that if I'd have been there to see it, my blood would have run cold. 'I'm liking you more and more every day, girl.'

Bullets smashed into the walls and through windows. Emily shouted a warning and Meredith rushed to a window and looked out. A rider with a torch approached the house and threw it onto the roof.

Ma cursed out loud and shot the hooded man in the back as he retreated. Meredith sighted along the barrel on a rider she hoped was Hardin. She fired and saw the man lurch in the saddle. He grasped at the saddle horn to keep himself upright.

The firing continued and the flames on the roof began to take hold. Slowly, smoke drifted down and inside the house.

'We have to get out of here!' Emily shouted. 'It's on fire!'

Meredith shot at another mounted rider and pulled away from the window. She called across to Emily. 'Help Blaze!'

Emily helped him towards the back door while Ma and Meredith kept up their steady rate of fire. The smoke grew thicker and they both began to cough.

'Come on, Mer,' Ma said. 'Out the back with you.'

'Damn bastards,' Meredith cursed. 'I wish Trace was here.'

'Me too; now out.'

They hurried out the back and hid near the barn. Taking hold even further, the night was soon lit a bright orange by the conflagration.

Emily said, 'Oh, Ma, the house. What will we do?'

'Don't worry about the house, girl,' she said in her usual gruff tone. 'We can rebuild that. But if that son of a bitch Deavers thinks he can get away with this, he's wrong.'

'What are you going to do, Elmira?' Meredith asked.

'I'm going to move us all to town and get Trace out of jail. Then I'm going to turn him loose on them bastards with my blessing. This has gone on for long enough.'

It took another hour for the nightriders to leave. They waited until the ranch house was well alight and gathered their dead and wounded. Then once they were gone, Meredith, Ma, Blaze and Emily emerged. The wagon was hitched and they came to town.

Early that morning, just after the sun had risen in the east, the wagon rumbled along the street and came to a halt outside of the boarding house where Ruby and Jordy were staying.

They unloaded Blaze and went in to the foyer where they were met by an elderly woman with a maddened expression on her face.

'Elmira Madden,' she chided, 'what is the meaning of this?'

'Ain't got time to bandy words with you, Penelope. I need a room for this man.'

'Why, you're all in your nightclothes. This . . . this hussy here has hardly anything on at all.'

It was then that Meredith realized the reason for her chilled skin. The boarding house owner was right, but Mer wasn't about to let the woman get away with calling her a hussy. Her face hardened and she snapped, 'Listen here, grandma. We had a damned house burned down around our ears by nightriding sons of bitches last night, so I'm in no mood for your horseshit. See this Winchester in my hand? I used it to kill at least one of them fellers last night, and right about now I don't care if I shoot me another person. And the next time you call me a hussy I'll do just that.'

Penelope's lined face paled and Ma gave her a smile. 'About that room, Penelope?'

It was about then that Ruby appeared at the top of the stairs.

'What's going on?' she demanded.

'They burned the ranch house last night,' Ma told her.

'Oh, Lord.'

'That's just where some of them fellers went, although I'm sure it might have been down instead of up,' Ma said.

'And they stole your cattle, too. When will this all end?'

'It'll end just as soon as Trace gets out of jail and unloads on them,' Ma growled. She turned back to the boarding house owner. 'The room, Penelope.'

CHAPTER 16

When Ma and Meredith came to the jail, Bannon had just given me a breakfast of eggs and beans. The eggs were baked up and the beans were dry. I stared at him and said, 'You ain't much at cooking, are you?'

'You don't have to eat it.'

'I really don't think I want to.'

Bannon took the food away. I said, 'The next time Ma comes in, I'll have them get us something to eat. Can't have you poison yourself with that stuff.'

'It's done me no harm so far.'

'That's your opinion.'

He grunted and started to eat the food himself. I winced, half expecting him to go tocs up then and there.

'How's the sheriff?' I asked him.

Bannon nodded. 'He's doing OK. Doc said he might actually pull through.'

'Good. I'm glad.'

The marshal stared at me, deep in thought. Then he asked, 'Tell me something. Why did you take on

131

the badge after he was shot?'

'He asked me to do it before he was shot,' I informed him.

'Before?'

'Uh-huh.'

'Why?'

'Why not?'

'You're an outlaw. The law ain't your thing. You usually run from it.'

'My sister has a thing for him. I couldn't let him get killed now, could I?'

'And yet he almost did.'

I nodded. 'Let's hope he learns from it.'

'You could have left, you know. I take it that young Harper told you a marshal was coming?'

'He did. But Deavers had my brother killed and I owe him for that. Besides, Ma couldn't fight this on her own.'

'You're damned right there.'

I stared over at the doorway through the bars and saw Ma and Meredith standing there. Both were armed, and their weapons were aimed at Bannon.

'What is this?' he asked.

Ma said, 'What do you think?'

'You mean to break your son out?'

Ma nodded. 'We had visitors last night. Burned my ranch house they did.'

Bannon stiffened at the news. 'Tell me what happened.'

I cursed under my breath. 'Is everyone OK, Ma? Mer, are you OK?'

Meredith nodded. 'I'm fine.'

'Yeah, but there's a few of them nightriders who ain't. They might've set fire to the house, but we put some lead in their hides while they was at it.'

'Get me out of here, Ma. The keys are on the hook.'

Meredith grabbed them down and opened the cell door. I looked at Bannon and gave him an option. 'You can help me, or you get locked up. Your choice.'

'I can't just let you go.'

I stepped aside, and he walked into the cell. The door closed behind him with a loud clang.

'Someone will keep an eye on you, Bannon. Might even get you some decent food.'

For a man in his predicament, he gave me a wry smile. 'That would be nice.'

I located my Colt and buckled it on. Then I found the Winchester and took a box of cartridges from a drawer, then a sawn-off shotgun came from the gun rack. Meredith watched me and then asked, 'Do you need some help?'

'From who?' I knew what she meant.

'Me.'

'You take care of Ma and the others. I've got this.'

She moved in close and kissed me on the cheek. She whispered in my ear. 'You make sure you come back to me.'

As I walked towards the door Bannon called out, 'You can't do this, Madden.'

I stopped and turned. 'Outlaw, remember?'

I didn't know it at the time, but as I left the jail, I

133

was being watched.

The smell of burnt wood still hung thick in the air as
I rode into the ranch yard. I cursed under my breath
as I stared at the smouldering ruin. My ma and pa
had worked so hard to build this up to what it had
been, and this was all that remained.

Climbing down from the horse, I walked about the
yard and stared at the horse tracks and bloodstains.
Then with it all etched in my mind, I remounted and
rode out of the yard. Someone was going to pay and
the first would be Cleve Hardin.

Not long after I had left the jail and Ma and
Meredith had gone to the boarding house, Bannon
received another visitor.

The marshal looked up from where he was seated
on the bunk and saw the newcomer enter. He said,
'Good. Open this door, can you? The keys are on the
hook there.'

And that's what the visitor did: took down the keys
and opened the door. Bannon thanked the person as
he walked through. And then the visitor shot him in
the back.

They left by the back door without first checking
to see if Bannon was dead. He wasn't, but at that time
it didn't matter. He was in no shape to talk, and in all
probability would die.

Most important of all, it had been made to look
like a jailbreak. And the last person in that cell had
been me.

'Marshal Bannon has been shot!' Emily exclaimed as she burst into Meredith's room.

Ma and Meredith whirled about. 'What?'

'It happened a short time ago. They're blaming Trace for it.'

'But that's just not true,' Ma said. 'He's been long gone.'

'But they don't know that,' Meredith pointed out. 'They don't know that we busted him out of there.'

Ma said, 'It doesn't matter though, does it? With the marshal dead they're not going to believe us.'

'He's not dead,' Emily blurted out. 'He's not good though. He could die.'

Meredith said, 'We need to find out who shot him.'

'How?' asked Emily.

'To find it out, we need to find out why.'

'Who would want to shoot him?' Emily asked. 'The only thing he's done since he got here was lock Trace up.'

'There is one other thing,' Ma said. 'The man Trace told him about. Heath.'

'The oil man?' Meredith queried.

'He's the only one I can think of.'

'How are we going to find out?' asked Emily.

Meredith smiled. 'By being nice.'

'Don't do anything foolish, girl,' Ma cautioned her.

CHAPTER 17

I followed the trail for a fair piece before it split into two. I knew where the first was going, but not the second. That was the one I followed, all the way to the line shack where Hardin and his two remaining men were hiding out.

As I was in no rush, I decided to watch and wait until dark. Reasonably sure at least one of them was wounded, probably gravely, I knew they weren't going anywhere. But I was. I wasn't here to bring Hardin and his men in. I was here to kill them. All of them.

I loaded the shotgun and settled in to wait. The sun sank slowly in the west, and once it had disappeared I started towards the shack on foot. This would be short and bloody. They should never have killed my friends and burned the ranch house. Deavers and Caldwell would be next.

This wasn't a job for the law. It had gone beyond that.

As I approached the shack, my footfalls on the rocky ground seemed excessively loud, almost deafening, and my heart hammered in my chest. Not from fear but with concern that someone would emerge from inside and see me.

The flimsy timber door flew back as my foot crashed against it and revealed a dimly lit room beyond. There was a loud curse and the sound of a chair falling over.

Stepping through the door I was confronted by one of Hardin's men. The hammers on the shotgun fell and almost cut him in half. The roar thundered inside the small room and the muzzle blast illuminated the area better than the candle on the plank table.

I discarded the shotgun and drew my Peacemaker. It came up in one fluid motion and I shot the man who had been seated at the table but lurched to his feet when the door burst open.

The .45 slug punched into his chest just above the white bandage hidden beneath his shirt. He cried out and stumbled backward over his chair with a crash.

That left Hardin, and I couldn't see him anywhere. My eyes glanced about the room. Nope, definitely not there, which meant—

I lunged forward out of the doorway just as the gun crashed behind me. The son of a bitch had been outside when I'd shot his two men and had escaped the first onslaught. It almost cost me my life.

Pain jarred through my body as I hit the floor and

then rolled out of the doorway. More bullets flew through the opening and slapped into the wall across the other side of the room.

'Madden! Is that you, Madden?'

The shout was hoarse with anger.

'Yeah, it's me, Hardin. Come on in and you can join your friends.'

'You're dead, Madden.'

Angry outlaw killers always say that. I think it is something they use to scare folks. 'How about we do this one on one, Hardin? Straight up, you and me.'

'Why would I do that?'

'You scared, killer? Getting yellow without your friends to back your play?'

Silence.

Hopefully I'd made him angrier than he already was. Angry men have the tendency to do silly things.

Which he did. He stormed through that door firing so wildly that the ceiling was in more danger than what I was.

I fired three times. Once was enough, as the first bullet from my Colt tore through his throat and sprayed blood everywhere. However, I wasn't happy with that. While he stood there as stiff as a board, his brain processing that he was dead, I fired twice more. Both slugs hammered into the killer's chest and he toppled over backward.

Staring down at Hardin's corpse, I felt no emotion whatsoever. Maybe I would have felt satisfied if there weren't more men to kill and the whole situation was over.

I replaced the spent rounds in my Colt with fresh loads and holstered it, then did the same with the shotgun and rested it upon my shoulder.

The candle on the table still burned and I picked it up. Then an idea came to me.

CHAPTER 18

'It was wonderful of you to dine with me this evening, Mr Heath. I must say I enjoyed your company immensely. Better than some of the scatterbrained men this town has to offer. There is nothing like dining with an educated gentleman.'

Heath gave her a warm smile. 'It's been my pleasure, Miss Blake. May I escort you anywhere?'

The two stood on the boardwalk outside of the café. The evening was cool but not unpleasant and there was a full moon. Meredith reached out and touched his hand. 'It's such a lovely night; it seems a shame to waste it.'

Heath offered her his arm and Meredith took it. 'I think that would be a tremendous idea.'

Meredith giggled.

'What's so funny?'

'That word you just used.'

'Tremendous?'

'Yes. Around here most of the men I know wouldn't

be able to spell half of it let alone say it.'

'Tremendous,' he said again with a smile.

And on cue, Meredith giggled.

They walked towards the edge of the town and stopped when the boardwalk ran out. Along the way they chatted about everything and anything that took their fancy, from Meredith's childhood to Heath's job. Not that he let on much at all. He just told her he worked for a company in Pennsylvania that required him to travel a lot.

Then things got kind of serious.

'It was a shame about the marshal getting shot,' Meredith said.

Heath nodded. 'I heard he wasn't long for this world.'

'It's hard to say. I was over at the doctor's, visiting him earlier, and he said he was in and out all of the time. Mumbling things.'

'Did he say who shot him?'

'Not yet. But wouldn't it be good if he did?'

'Yes. Yes, it would.'

'Oh, that reminds me: I have to go and see Doctor Grace before he goes for supper. The poor man doesn't get much of a break of late with the sheriff as well. I'm sorry, but I must cut our walk short.'

'No, no. By all means,' Heath said graciously. 'Would you like an escort?'

'No, thank you, kind sir. I'll be able to find my way.'

'Shall I see you tomorrow, perhaps?' Heath asked.

141

She smiled at him. 'I'd like that.'

Heath stood and watched Meredith leave. Then he went too.

The door to the room where Bannon lay unconscious swung open at a gentle speed. It made no sound and when it stopped, a figure stepped through the opening.

It walked slowly towards the comatose lawman and stopped. A hand reached into a coat and drew a long, thin-bladed knife. It was raised above Bannon and made ready to plunge down when the figure stopped and turned.

'I knew it was you, you son of a bitch.' Meredith said in a cold voice.

Heath stared down at the Colt in her hand. He lowered the knife and smiled at her. Then his expression changed, and he took a step forward.

The six-gun in Meredith's small fist roared and the slug slammed into the oil man's chest. His jaw dropped in shock as the wet patch on his chest began to grow. He lurched forward a few steps and reached out to Meredith with shaky hands, trying to use her for support.

All he got from her was another bullet in his chest.

Ma and Doc Grace entered the room and stared down at the corpse. Meredith turned to face the old medic and said, 'I'm sorry about the mess on your floor.'

'Never you mind that, girl. At least now the town will know the truth about who the real culprit is and

not blame Trace.'
   'No . . . not . . . not Trace.'
   Bannon was awake.

CHAPTER 19

The fire burned bright against the night sky and small embers floated into the darkness on the updraft. I remained outside the perimeter of firelight and waited patiently for the riders I knew would come. And they did. Two of them.

I heard some muttered curses and something about Hardin. When I stepped out of the shadows with the sawn-off trained on them, they were none too happy.

'Madden! Son of a bitch,' one of them cursed.

'I am,' I conceded. 'But you have me at a disadvantage. Who might you be?'

'Chuck Williams.'

My brain ticked over. 'I remember you.'

'Yeah?'

'Yeah. Smart Alec son of a bitch who always thought he was better than the next guy.'

'Did you start this fire?' the other man asked.

'I did.'

'You know you're trespassing on Broken D land?'

'I do.'

In the glow of the fire I could see the pained expression on each of their faces from restraining themselves from asking the obvious question. Instead, I made it easy for them. I said, 'I killed them.'

'What?' said Williams.

'Hardin and his men. They're in there,' I pointed at the fire.

'You burned them?'

'After I shot them.'

They went silent.

'My turn,' I said. 'Where are the cattle?'

'What cattle?' Williams sneered.

My Colt came out in a blur and I shot him. I didn't kill him, just put a hunk of lead in his hide where it would cause him the most agony for a while. The fact that he fell from his horse was a bonus.

He howled with pain and then screeched at me, 'You bastard. You damned well shot me.'

Ignoring him, I moved my point of aim to his friend. 'The cows.'

He spilled his guts before I could do it for him. I thanked him and said, 'I want you to go to town and tell the marshal what happened here.'

He looked at me all weird. 'What?' I asked.

He just stared at me.

'Out with it, damn it.'

'You shot the marshal this morning when you escaped jail.'

The words hit me harder than any bullet could.

'The hell I did. Who said that?'

'It's all over town.'

Stampeding thoughts overwhelmed my mind and I reeled backwards. Then came the realization that there was absolutely nothing I could do about it at that moment. I said, 'Go back to Deavers and tell the son of a bitch I'm coming for him.'

'Good luck with that,' he snorted.

'What's that supposed to mean?'

'He's got the woman and kid.'

'He what?' Meredith gasped.

'I saw Mr Deavers walk out of here around lunch time with Ruby and the boy,' Penelope offered.

Meredith cursed loudly, and shock registered on Penelope's face.

'This is bad,' Ma said.

'He left a letter for you, Elmira.'

'Now why didn't you say that before?' Ma scolded her.

'I forgot.'

Penelope handed it over and Ma read it. Her face paled, then reddened. 'Why that low-down, dirty rotten bastard,' Ma cursed out loud. 'I'll kill that son of a bitch myself.'

'Well, I never . . .' Penelope started indignantly.

'Oh, shut up!' Ma snapped. 'Mer, he says that if I don't hand over the ranch to him, he'll kill them both.'

'What are you going to do?'

'What can I do?'

Meredith turned away from Ma and started

146

towards the door.

'Where are you going?'

'To find Trace.'

'It's the middle of the night.'

'Then I better hope I don't miss him.'

Caldwell entered Deavers' study and stood in front of his desk. 'We've got another problem.'

'Trace Madden?'

The gunman nodded. 'He killed Hardin and his men. Burnt the shack down with their bodies in it.'

'How do we know this?'

'Williams and Borden just rode in. Williams is carrying lead that Madden put in him.'

Deavers' face turned grim. 'I see.'

'He asked them about the cattle.'

'I take it that they told him?'

'Under threat of death, yeah. He also knows you've got the woman and the boy.'

Deavers reached across his desk and picked up a half-full brandy decanter. He pulled the stopper and poured a glass.

After taking a sip he stared at Caldwell and asked, 'You think he'll come after them?'

Caldwell nodded. 'Yeah.'

'Then we can kill him. The last damned thorn in my side.'

The gunman wasn't so sure.

'What is it?'

'The women are tougher than you give them credit for.'

'We'll see. Have the men get ready. No one sleeps. I don't want Madden slipping in here in the dark and getting the drop on us.'

Caldwell nodded. 'I'll roust them out.'

CHAPTER 20

I waited until daylight to move on the Broken D ranch house. I was sure that Deavers would have his men up half of the night after being informed by his men that I would be coming. The longer I waited, the tireder they'd be, and fatigued men make mistakes.

I sat atop my horse on a rise that overlooked the Broken D ranch house. There was plenty of movement in the yard. Men posted like sentries around the perimeter, waiting for me to arrive.

It would be almost impossible for me to get in there unnoticed. So, I kept them waiting even longer.

The sound of hoofbeats sent my heart racing but when I turned and saw who it was, it slowed some.

'What are you doing here?' I snapped.

It wasn't the reception she'd been expecting but Meredith took it in her stride. 'I was looking for you. He's got Ruby and Jordy.'

'I know.'

149

She stared at me for a moment then asked, 'Are you OK?'

'Yeah.'

'Are you sure?'

'Yeah. Go back to town.'

'Why?'

I remained silent.

Then the realization hit her. 'You're not going down there, are you?'

'Yes.'

'Trace, no.'

'Someone has to. There's no law to do it.'

'They'll kill you.'

I could hear the anxiety in her voice. 'I'm a hard man to kill, Mer.'

'Damn you, Trace Madden,' she hissed.

'Probably.'

'How're the marshal and Jeff?' I asked.

'The doc said they'll both live.'

I nodded. 'Good.'

'I shot the oil man.'

I slowly turned my head to face the woman I loved more than life itself. 'You what?'

'He shot the marshal, so I shot him.'

'Well, that'll throw a burr under someone's saddle.'

'The main thing is that people will know that it wasn't you who shot Bannon. Give me your gun.'

I frowned at her.

'If you ride down into that yard, they'll shoot you down. Agreed?'

I shrugged my shoulders. 'More than likely.'

'What if I go down there?'

'No.'

'Just listen, Trace. Gideon Blake, or whatever name he's using now, doesn't want me dead. Only you. If I can get in there and hold him at gunpoint, maybe stir things up a little so that they're all looking the other way, then maybe you will stand a chance.'

I didn't like it. Not at all. But my way involved me dying, of that I was pretty sure. There was still one problem. 'What about Ruby and Jordy?'

'Maybe I can get us all in one room.'

'If I agree to this, Mer, you promise me one thing.'

'Anything.'

'If you get into trouble, don't put up a fight. I don't want you getting hurt.'

'Only if I can put a bullet in that bastard first.'

I shook my head and took the Peacemaker from my holster. 'Why not?'

The hands from the Broken D sure got a surprise when Meredith rode into the yard. I'm sure that in all their lives they'd never seen a young woman as pretty as she is, but I guess I'm kind of partial to her.

Anyway, they all gathered around her, and one of them even helped her from her mount. From where I sat I could imagine her giving them all her best smile and a wink here and there. Then I saw Caldwell emerge onto the veranda, and Meredith passed her reins over to the nearest hand and went inside.

Then I started to ride down the rise.

151

'What do you want?'

'I'm here to see Gideon.'

Caldwell stared at her with suspicion. Then he said, 'Come on in.'

When Meredith entered the house she asked Caldwell, 'Where are Ruby and the boy?'

Without turning, he said, 'They're safe.'

She let it go.

The gunman showed her into Deavers' study and he said, 'You have a visitor.'

Deavers looked up and immediately came to his feet. 'Meredith? It's you.'

'Hello, Gideon.'

'What. . . . It's good to see you.'

'I wish I could say the same. Where is the woman and the boy?'

'Still the same. Straight to the point.'

She nodded. 'Still the same, Gideon. Do whatever it takes to get what you want. Only this time you've bitten off more than you can chew.'

'You mean Madden?'

'Uh-huh.'

'He won't be around for much longer.'

Meredith ignored his comment and walked across to the window and looked outside. She stared at the men in the yard and then turned around. When she did, she had the Colt in her fist and the hammer drawn back.

Deavers got over his initial shock and gave

Meredith a mirthless smile. 'What now, Mer? Do you intend to shoot me?'

He chuckled drily and shook his head. But Meredith wasn't in a joking mood. She shrugged her shoulders and said, 'No.'

Then she shot Caldwell. Blam! Blam! Blam! Three times in the chest. The hired gun went down before he could even get his gun out.

Meredith swivelled and trained the Colt on Deavers' guts and hissed, 'Move and you'll get the same, you son of a bitch.'

'What the hell are you doing?' Deavers snarled.

'Ending it once and for all.'

Hearing the shots, I ground my teeth together and heeled the horse forward. Under the circumstances, I failed to take in the breathtaking scenery around me that was the Broken D ranch. In my left hand was the sawn-off shotgun and in my right was the Winchester. I used my knees to guide my mount, which responded to the gentle pressure.

When we thundered into the yard, all the hands were confused, their focus being directed towards the house. They'd heard gunfire from inside and were trying to work out what was going on.

Suddenly one of them turned around at the sound of hoofbeats and shouted a warning.

To get where I needed to be I knew I'd need some luck. Whether I received it or not remained to be seen.

I came out of the saddle as soon as the warning was

shouted. There were ten of them, I think. I'm not sure. Although when the shotgun discharged with its throaty roar, there were two less.

Casting it aside, the Winchester came into play before they could recover. I fired it and a third man fell beside the other two. The rest now brought their weapons to bear as they scattered in all directions.

A bullet kicked up the dirt at my feet, fired by a man who'd taken shelter behind a water trough. I fired back at him just as he poked his head up to take another shot. The bullet smashed into his head, killing him instantly.

I levered another round into the breech and felt the tug of a slug as it clipped the sleeve of my coat. The shooter stood on the veranda with only a post to hide behind. I fired and the bullet smashed into one leg that was protruding enough to make a perfect target.

He howled in pain and tumbled to the timber planks beneath him. I worked the lever and shot him again.

A loud snap made me duck slightly as a round passed close by my head. The gunman was on one knee on the veranda to the left of the other three who'd fallen there. He was sighting along his rifle for another shot when I fired.

He hunched over as the slug from the Winchester ripped into his guts. The flattened hunk of lead then tore through everything it touched and exploded out of his back to the right of his spine.

I felt the burn of a bullet score a furrow in my

upper left arm. I flinched as I fired, and my next shot flew wide of its intended target. I jacked another round into the Winchester and fired at the gunman who'd moved to a flatbed wagon beside the house. I shot him in the chest, levered and shot a man next to him who collapsed when the bullet flew low and smashed his lower leg.

It couldn't last. It wouldn't be long before one of these hired guns actually shot straight enough to put me down. I kept walking towards the front door of the house. Out of the corner of my eye I caught a glimpse of another gun about to fire and I turned at the hip. I levered and fired three times and splinters flew from the wagon as they were gouged from the seat.

Then something quite unexpected happened. The man threw up his arms and surrendered. Followed by another, and another.

All of those who remained simply gave up and ceased firing. It was bizarre. Maybe no one else was willing to die for their boss.

A quick head-count and I could see why. Only four remained. I stared at one of them and said, 'Get the hell out of here.'

They didn't need to be told twice. All of them ran towards the corral.

After making sure they were gone, I turned on my heel and started towards the door. Who knew what I would find inside?

CHAPTER 21

'You hear that?' Deavers snarled. 'He's dead. My men have killed him. Now what are you going to do, bitch?'

Meredith's mind reeled as she tried to process it all. Could it be true? Could Trace be dead? No. Not Trace. He always had a way of coming through. She wouldn't believe it. Couldn't.

Deavers' voice changed. 'Give me the gun, Mer.'

She stared at him, the expression on her face a mixture of confusion and pain.

He held out his right hand. 'Give me the gun.'

Meredith didn't move.

Deavers heard footfalls approaching from outside the door. Then came the voice. 'Meredith?'

Her eyes widened at the sound of Trace's voice. Deavers, however, shared no such feelings and suddenly produced a small hideout gun from beneath his sleeve.

*

The sound of gunfire from beyond the door spurred me into action. My shoulder hit the wood panel and it sprang wide. On the other side, I saw Deavers and Meredith. She had her back to me and when I looked at the Broken D boss I saw the derringer in his hand.

I raised the rifle to fire but saw him stagger. Not much, just a shuffle to the left. Then he opened his mouth to say something, but all that escaped his lips was a wet gurgle and a torrent of bright-red blood.

Like a giant tree Deavers fell to the floor. On his way down, he hit the edge of his desk and skittered the chair backwards.

I hurried to Meredith's side. 'Are you OK?'

She nodded dumbly. 'I killed him.'

I saw the Colt still in her grasp. It trembled along with the rest of her body. I reached out and took it from her. 'I can see that. Come on, let's go find Ruby and the boy.'

Suddenly it was as though Meredith was seeing me for the first time. She threw her arms around me. 'Trace, you're still alive.'

I wrapped her up in a tight hug. 'Yes, Mer. I'm still alive.'

Then she buried her face into my shoulder and cried.

We stood like that for a few minutes and then she pulled away, wiping her eyes and nose with her hand.

'Are you OK?' I asked her again.

She nodded. 'Let's go and find Ruby.'

We found them in a spare room, unharmed and

relieved to see us. After more hugs and tears, we all headed back to town.

I eased my horse up to the hitchrail outside the jail and stared down at the man who sat in a chair on the boardwalk. He stared back and asked, 'You all ready to go?'

I glanced back along the street and saw the wagon coming, Ma on the seat. She slapped the reins across the backs of the four-horse team and said a few choice words. Beside her sat Ruby and squeezed between them was Jordy. Behind the wagon rode Meredith, Blaze, Emily and Jeff.

Looking back to Bannon, I said, 'Yeah, I think that's everyone.'

The wagon rattled to a halt behind me.

'Can't say I'll be sad to see the back of you, Trace. Just do me one thing: when you get to wherever it is you're going, stay out of trouble.'

Meredith eased her horse in beside mine. 'His outlaw days are all done, Marshal.'

He smiled at her. 'Never did thank you for what you did. Even though you busted your man here out of jail.'

She smiled back at him. 'I'd do it all again.'

'I believe you would.'

'Are you lot going to keep flapping your gums for the rest of the day, or what? If you're going to lock him up, Marshal, just do it. It would serve him right.'

Yep, Ma sure has a way with words.

Bannon chuckled. 'You'd best get going before

she climbs down and takes a switch to you.'

I nodded. 'She's likely to do it, too. Between her and Meredith I reckon I'll have my work cut out for me.'

'You want me to shoot you again?'

Bannon raised a quizzical eyebrow. I said, 'Long story.'

'Oh.'

'Yeah.'

'Well, I'll be seeing you, Trace.'

I eased my horse away from the hitchrail and touched a finger to my hat brim. Then I said, 'Mer.'

She smiled at Bannon and shook her head. 'Sorry, Marshal, but no, you won't.'